A Lady

Evening Recreations

A Collection of Original Stories : For the Amusement of her Young Friends

A Lady

Evening Recreations
A Collection of Original Stories : For the Amusement of her Young Friends

ISBN/EAN: 9783744750257

Printed in Europe, USA, Canada, Australia, Japan

Cover: Foto ©Andreas Hilbeck / pixelio.de

More available books at **www.hansebooks.com**

EVENING RECREATIONS:

A

COLLECTION

OF

ORIGINAL STORIES,

For the amusement of her

YOUNG FRIENDS,

BY A LADY.

LONDON:

PRINTED FOR J. DEIGHTON, NO. 325, HOLBORN.

MDCCXCIV.

TABLE

OF

CONTENTS.

---

a   dif-

STORY III.

STORY IV.

EVENING RECREATIONS.

STORY I

AT a village in Hampſhire, lived a very worthy gentleman of the name of Alworthy, who devoted the chief of his time to the education of his children.

One morning he invited his ſon Edmond to accompany him in a

B   walk

walk to the New Foreſt ; they ſtood for ſome time attentively watching an old man who was employed felling one of the largeſt oaks ; poor fellow, ſaid Edmond, it is a ſad thing for him to be obliged to ſlave ſo hard in his old age ; by no means, replied Mr. Alworthy, whilſt Providence bleſſes him with health ; for you ſee he has none of the infirmities of old age upon him ; well, papa, ſaid Edmond, but it is a ſhocking thing to be poor ! the extreme of poverty, replied his father, is doubtleſs ſhock-ing ; but you ſeem to have taken up a falſe idea upon the diſtinctions that Providence has allotted in ſociety. A good man, whatever may be his

misfor-

misfortunes in life, can never be com-
pletely miferable; and the rectitude
of his own heart will fupport him
through the moft trying fituations!
there is, my dear boy, implanted in
our breafts an innate principle of
right and *wrong*, and young as you
are, you doubtlefs have felt it:
What I mean is, that when your
conduct has been praife-worthy, you
have felt a degree of fatisfaction in
your own mind that told you, you
had acted right; and a fenfation
the reverfe of this, you have ex-
perienced whenever you have done
wrong, and this is what we term
confcience; and even allowing that
the woodman, was reduced from

.   B 2   affluence,

affluence, to labour for his daily fupport, yet, if his poverty was neither
the effect of extravagance or folly,
he would not be miferable, for his
mind would rife fuperior to the
diftrefs of his fituation.

To every ftation in life Providence has kindly allotted a propor-
tionate degree of happinefs: and the
heart of the peafant is as fufceptable
of tendernefs as the heart of the
prince. Perhaps, could we follow
the old man to his humble abode,
we fhould there witnefs a fcene that
might convince us, he was rather an
object of envy than pity; we might
fee him bleffed with a faithful partner

in

in life, whofe unwearied affection and
perfevering induftry, had rendered
her dearer to him than when they
were firft united ; we might fee
him furrounded by a numerous off-
fpring of children and grand children,
emulous to gratify his wifhes ! we
might obferve that this man poffeffed a heart contented at its own fituation, nor repined at the fuperiority of
his neighbours; and fhall we fay fuch
a man as this is unhappy, becaufe
he is poor ? Oh no, papa, faid Edmond, I do not know how it was,
but I always thought poor people
muft be miferable ! When ficknefs
befalls the poor, replied Mr. Alworthy, they inftantly become objects

of the greateſt compaſſion, and it
then becomes the *duty* of the *rich*, not
only to compaſſionate their ſufferings,
but relieve them; for, I think charity one of the faireſt of the Chriſtian
virtues; and I am ſure it is one that
carries with it its own reward, for of
all the delightful ſenſations of which
our nature is capable, none is ſo gra-
tifying to a feeling mind as that ari-
ſing from the reflection of having mi-
tigated the ſufferings of a fellow-crea-
ture.

At this moment the woodman joined them; well Sir, ſaid he, I got
through it mortal well, for an old
man, did not I? Why, my friend,
ſaid

said Mr. Alworthy, that arm of your's has given many a sturdy stroke. Ah, lack-a-day, that it has—Why, please your honour, I have worked at this business five-and-fifty years, and no man ever said Will Wiggins's arm could not lower the stoutest timber amongst them; and I hope I shall down with many another yet, Sir, for I don't desire to die, though I am an old man; for I have got those about me worth living for: I have got, Sir, a good old dame for a wife, and five sons, all as worthy lads as e'er an old man was blessed with; but please your honour, what is it o'clock? for this is our wedding-day, and I pro-mised my old lady to be at home by

twelve,

twelve, for fhe is got plum-pudding and baked beef, and my fons, their wives, and all their little ones, are to dine with us, and I intend to dance with my youngeft grandchild. Then take that, my honeft friend, faid Mr. Alworthy, putting five fhillings into his hand, and drink to the happy return of many a wedding-day.

Well Edmond, faid Mr. Alworthy, you have now had an opportunity of judging whether the account I gave you of the bleffings attendant upon an humble fituation, were exaggerated; why, indeed papa, Wiggins feems fo very happy, that I could almoft wifh I was to be a woodman; my

dear

dear boy remember, that the firſt eſſential ſtep towards happineſs, is *content*. Whatever may be your ſtation in life, habituate your mind to view it on its faireſt ſide, nor ever allow yourſelf to think that the grapes on your neighbours vine, yield a richer flavor than thoſe on your own.

Pray papa, ſaid Edmond, looking at the immenſe tree that Wiggins's proweſs had levelled with the duſt, are not oaks the largeſt trees that grow ? No, replied Mr. Alworthy, the oak ſinks as much when compared with the calabaſh tree, as a ſhrub does when compared to a oak ;

it

it is the largeſt known vegetable production, and is a native of Senegal in Africa; the negros dry the bark and leaves and then reduce them to a powder, and take it medicinally as a preventative to the fever common in that country.

Talking of medicine, is rhubarb a tree papa? no, replied Mr. Alworthy, it is a plant chiefly brought from the eaſtern part of Tartary, but it is the root of the plant that is valuable. I think papa, ſaid Edmond, I ſhould like, if you would teach me botany, that I might know the uſe of every vegetable that grows; that would be taking botany upon a very large ſcale my

my dear fellow, though a very humane one.

As they were converfing, Edmond
obferved a ftag whofe antlers had got
entangled in the boughs of a tree,
oh papa, faid he, do but look, if
you had but a gun we might live
upon venifon for a week.   It would
be rather cowardly, furely Edmond,
faid. Mr. Alworthy, to attack the
poor animal in that helplefs fituation.
I believe we fhall feel more pleafure
in affifting it to regain its liberty,
than we fhould to fee it ftruggling in
the agonies of death, by the de-
ftructive power of our fire arms ; and
therefore let us haften to difengage it.
                                        I never

I never, continued Mr. Alworty, fee thefe animals without its calling to my remembrance the infinite good-nefs of our Creator in forming an animal of that fpecies, poffeffing powers from which man derives fuch effential benefits ; for, to the Lap-lander, the rain deer fupplies the place of every other ufeful animal : by its food he is fupported, by its milk regaled, with its fkin he is clothed, and by its fpeed he is tranf-ported with a degree of fwftnefs in-conceivable over the icy plains. Well papa, faid Edmond, don't you think the Laplanders mufl a be very mifer-able fet of creatures ? not miferable, my dear boy, replied Mr. Alworthy, but

but pitiable; the extreme feverity
of their climate, and the hardinefs of
their lives, joined to the very few
comforts attendant upon their ftation,
muft make every feeling mind com-
paffionate fuch a fituation. Yet you
are to recollect that they never new
any other, and thofe bleffings we
have no idea of, we can never figh
after! and if the Laplander is incapable of refined pleafures, reft affured
he has the power of enjoying rational
ones : and whilft he poffeffes a faithful wife, affectionate children, and a
fincere friend, depend upon it he can
never be a miferable creature. Why
papa, faid Edmond, you talk as if
every body was happy in the world,
                                    and

and yet I have heard a great deal about the misery of it ; no, Edmond, replied Mr. Alworthy, I mean not to imprefs you with an idea that we are all happy, for real happinefs is beyond the reach of mortality, and fortunate is it for us, that it is fo, or we fhould become fo delighted with this world, that we fhould never think of another ; but my dear boy, I wifh you to be convinced, that happinefs neither confifts in riches or honours, and that thofe people who appear moft to be envied, are often objects of pity. Well, papa, I don't underftand how that can be ; fuppofe for example, I was to loofe the affection of your mother, that you were to

prove

prove undutiful, and my friend false ; yet these are all circumstances I could not go and blazen forth to the world ; I should still have a fine house, fine coach, and a good estate, and the world would think me a happy man ; yet whose situation would be the most enviable, mine or the poor woodman's, who we saw this morning ? why, papa, the woodman's a great deal, but I hope none of these shocking things will happen to you ; I am not fearful they will, said Mr. Alworthy, and I only mentioned them to prove to you how very seldom we can judge of the happiness or misery of our fellow creatures from outward circumstances ; and we are

all

all fo differently formed by nature, that thofe events of life, that to one man appear ferious evils, to another are received merely as a bitter draught, to give a greater relifh to the fweets that follow ; but however, I hope you, my dear Edmond, will attain a degree of fortitude of mind that will enable you to bear the evils that may avait you, with compofure and calm refignation to the will of that Being who decreed them ; for reft affured none of us are exempt from trials of this nature; at the fame time not only receive the bleffings that are in ftore for you with gratitude, but cheerfulnefs, for they are given us for our enjoyment.

At

At this moment they were joined by Mrs. Alworthy and her youngeſt ſon; Charles and I, ſaid ſhe, really thought you intended ſpending the day in the foreſt, and fancying you muſt have found ſomething very agreeable here, we were determined to come and partake of it. Whatever was the cauſe that brought you, ſaid Mr. Alworthy, the effect is very pleaſing to both Edmond and myſelf, and ſo take my arm and leave the boys to their own converſation. They had not walked a great way, when the two boys came running up to them, do papa, ſaid Edmond, look towards the ſea; what can occaſion that great fog to be confined to one

part

part of it? oh, replied **Mr. Alworthy**, I am very glad you have had the opportunity of witneffing the wonderful power of inftinct: that fog as you fancied it, is no other than an immenfe body of the feathered race winging their flight to a milder region; the fwallows, you are to know, are of too delicate a nature to endure the rigour of our winter, and therefore Providence has wifely implanted in their nature an inftinctive faculty that occafions them to collect in large bodies in the month of October and migrate to a fofter clime; but as foon as vernal fun's enliven the face of nature, thefe little wanderers again return, and this generally happens

pens in April. Come, faid Charles,
I want you, Edmond, to help me
pick up fome acorns, and away they
both ran for that purpofe; as they
were thus employed, they were addreffed by a beggar, a young healthy
looking man, dreffed as a foldier,
who folicited charity; he told them
a pitiable tale of diftrefs, and faid,
he had not eaten a morfel for eight-
and-forty hours, and that he had a
wife and children ftarving with hun-
ger; the boys inftantly put their
hands in their pockets, and between
them gave the man four-pence; heaven reward your charity, faid the
man; but my dear young gentlemen,
I fear my wife will die for want of

nou-

noürifhment, fhe has juft lain-in,
and this four-pence will not·buy
much; oh, but we have got a fhil-.
ling each, faid the children eagerly,
there take it, and run and procure
your poor wife a little wine to comfort her; the man inftantly turned
into a by-path and was out of fight
in a moment; foon after their father
and mother joined them, and Mr.
Alworthy propofed returning home,
as he recollected an appointment he
had made with a gentleman, but
promifed them another walk on the
following morning.

S T O R Y II.

THE next morning, as soon as breakfaft was over, the two boys repaired to the gardens to amufe themfelves with a game at trap-ball, and was foon after joined by Mr. and Mrs. Alworthy; well, faid the former;. I have not forgotten my yefterday's promife, are you inclined for a walk this morning? oh yes, papa, that we are, replied the boys, and the trap and ball were inftantly thrown afide; I think, faid Mr. Alworthy, buttoning

C 3. his.

his coat, we are going to have winter at a very early period, for I proteſt I could bear my great coat; why, ſaid Mrs. Alworthy, if you talk of a great coat now, we muſt procure you a Ruſſian peliſſe by Chriſtmas; a Ruſſian peliſſe, mamma, what is that? ſaid Charles; it is, my dear, returned his mother, a large fur cloak, that the Ruſſians wrap themſelves up in to defend themſelves againſt the rigours of their climate, and with this a cap, and boots of the ſame materials, they are proof againſt its ſeverity; but why, mamma, replied Charles, don't they were hats, inſtead of caps? becauſe, continued Mrs. Alworthy, the cold is ſo very intenſe, that if their ears were

not

not defended againſt its attacks, the effect would be dreadful; and it is no uncommon thing for them to be froſt-bitten; the mode of cure for this, is the rubbing them with ſnow, but if they came near a fire a mortifica- tion would be the certain conſe- quence; but in the year ſeventeen hundred and forty, the froſt was ſo very ſevere, that, at Peterſburgh, they built an intire palace of ice, and formed a rampart, from which they fired ſeveral ſhot from cannon formed of the ſame materials. Oh, replied Charles, I ſhould not like to live in Ruſſia, they muſt ſurely ſit over the fire all day long; very far from it, ſaid Mr. Alworthy, for when I was there,

which

which happened in the winter feafon, I affure you, I partook of all their amufements; I ufed to drive my fledge upon the Neva with as much bold-nefs as the natives, and flide down their ice hills with as little regard to the fafety of my neck; ice hills, papa, faid Edmond, is Ruffia a very hilly country? no, but the hills I mean are artificial ones, formed upon the river Neva, they are compofed of planks raifed between thirty and forty feet high and covered with ice. Thefe hills you afcend by the help of a ladder, and feating yourfelf in the fledge, it glides down with fuch amazing velocity, that it is often carried upwards of an hundred yards forward upon the plain.

plain. I think, papa, faid Edmond, the Neva is the largeſt river in Europe? no, the Volga is of ſuperior ſize, and is very near it.

Pray papa, faid Charles, is Peterſburgh a very fine place? yes, replied Mr. Alworthy, I think you would call it ſo, and when we conſider that at the beginning of this century it was a mere morafs and the habitation of a few fiſhermen only, it gives one a fine idea of the powers of art and induſtry, for the noblemens ſeats are magnificent, though upon the whole not quite ſo much ſo as thoſe at Mofcow. At Mofcow I was extremely aſtoniſhed by a gentleman calling upon

upon me one morning to invite me to go with him to the houſe-market; the houſe-market, papa, exclaimed Charles; yes, you are to know that the common peoples houſes are all of wood, and this market is a perfect ſtreet formed of movable ones, which in two or three days after the pur-chaſe, is thoroughly completed and inhabited.

Pray papa, ſaid Edmond, were you preſented to the Empreſs, for I heard her court was a very ſplendid one? to give you an exact idea of its mag-nificence is impoſſible, replied Mr. Alworthy, the Empreſs is more richly habited than you can conceive, and

adorned

adorned with a crown of diamonds; fhe is preceded and followed by a train of courtiers, who each feem to vie with the other in fplendour; but there is a moft beautiful fpot where the Emprefs often retires with a felect party of her friends, called the Hermitage, and once a week fhe gives a private ball and fupper there, fervants are wholly excluded; and the various refrefhments emerge through trap doors; but the Ruffians in general, though very hofpitable, are fond of a difplay of oftentation; and the poor, are a more dependant fet of beings than you can conceive; in fhort, there cannot be a more abject fet of creatures than a Ruffian peafant.

fant. I think, faid Mrs. Alworthy, upon the whole, the poor of our own country, are a happier fet of beings than in any other; doubtlefs they are fo, replied Mr. Alworthy, and the firft of bleffing is the liberty they enjoy; no abject fervility is here required, by the mafter from his fervants, his wants are all fupplied, and his comforts attended too; this fubject, continued Mrs. Alworthy, reminds me of the accident Molly has juft told me happened to Thomas Downing, and if you have no objection, we will walk and fee him; certainly, faid Mr. Alworthy, but how did it happen? I hear that as he was gathering apples yefter-day

day morning, he fell from the ladder and has broke his leg; as they arrived at the door of the cottage they met the furgeon coming out, and had the fatisfaction of hearing that there was no fymptom of danger attending the accident; he has but little fever, faid the furgeon, but this, I believe, is owing to his being fo very fober a man; for I never faw him in a public houfe in my life. They now entered the room where the fick man was confined, every thing wore an appearance of the greateft neatnefs, and his wife, boiling a little barley water, was fo very pretty, and fo delicately clean in her perfon, that Edmond could

not

not help going up to his mamma to beg she would look at her. Why, my poor fellow, said Mr. Alworthy, softening his voice and taking Thomas by the hand, I am sorry to see you thus; but however, have a good heart, and I don't doubt but I shall soon see you able to run and jump with the best cricket player in the village; I can bear pain, sir, said the man, but my poor Mary takes it so sadly to heart, and that is worse than all the rest, for there she stands, and she knows I have often told her, that I would walk ten miles after I was tired from work, rather than see her cry! and now she has done nothing else ever since I was brought home!

and

and I know fhe will make herfelf
fick, and God knows who is to nurfe
her! for though fhe looks fo rofy,
fhe cannot knock a man down as a
body may fay. Well, but my good
tender-hearted Mary, faid Mrs. Alworthy to her, it is very wrong to
give way to your own feelings, at the
hazard of hurting your poor hufband.
Hurting him, madam! God knows,
I would die to fave him from pain!
But when I fee him lay there, and
think that I may loofe him, I feel
almoft choaked with grief, and I
believe I fhould be quite fo, if I was
not to cry; this is all very natural,
my dear woman, continued Mrs.
Alworthy, but you fhould never dif-

truft

truſt the providence of God; and the ſurgeon tells me, that your huſband will do very well again, and we will do all we can to make you comfortable; you ſhall have your dinner from our table every day, and a little girl to nurſe your child, and I will pay her, that you may devote your whole time to your huſband, and when I call again in the evening, I ſhall expect Thomas, that you will give me a good account of her behaviour; ſaying this, Mrs. Alworthy hurried out of the room, as ſhe ſaw the poor creature was quite oppreſſed by her feelings of gratitude. Now my dear boys, ſaid Mr. Alworthy, as I wiſh to encourage the principles of true

true benevolence. I think the family
we have juſt left, are, during the ill-
neſs of poor Thomas, objects of real
charity : for you know his wages
muſt ceaſe from the time of the accident, therefore I would adviſe you
to put by a part of your weekly allowance, until he recovers, and then
give it him towards diſcharging his
ſurgeon's account, and as I know you
have money in your pockets, ſuppoſe
you let me be your banker ; we
ſhould be very happy to do it, papa,
ſaid the boys, but we really are
moneyleſs, and at the ſame time they
related the manner in which they had
diſpoſed of it. I ſhould be very ſorry,
replied Mr. Alworthy, to check the

D emotions

emotions of humanity in the breaft
of youth, yet I cannot help thinking
the man who was the object of your
charity was an impofture; furely,
papa, faid Edmond, that is judging
very harfhly, and what can be your
reafon for it ? why, in the firft place,
if he had really fafted eight and forty
hours, he would not have ftruck you
as looking fo very healthy, and befides your mother's humanity is fo
extenfive, that had any poor creature
been in the fituation he defcribed
his wife, fome one would have told
her, that her diftrefs might have
been relieved, had fhe made proper
application.

At

At this moment they were over-taken by a party of foldiers, and the identical object of the boys compaf-fion, walking hand-cuffed in the midft of them, uttering the moft abufive language to thofe around him; oh, papa, faid Edmond eagerly, that is the very man; well, replied Mr. Alworthy, let this be a caution to you to endeavour to diftinguifh between real and imaginary objects of diftrefs; yet never let it fuffer you to become fufpicious, or to check the amiable fenfation of compaffion, but only let it lead you to endea-vour not to fuffer your charity to be impofed on, for you are now with-held from doing an act of real kind-

nefs

nefs by having expended that money
upon a bad character that might
have added to the comfort of a good
one ; however, faid Mr. Alworthy,
we will now return home, and I fhall
be ready to devote the remaining
part of the morning to your ftudies,
which, faid Mrs. Alworthy, if you
acquit yourfelves in to the approbation of your father, you fhall accompany me in my evening walk to
Thomas Downing's.

STORY III.

CAPTAIN Harcourt was a gentleman in the naval line, and no lefs beloved and efteemed for his public character, than for his private virtues : Mrs. Harcourt united a fweetnefs of manners to a liberality of mind, and her heart was open to the moft refined impreffions of frendfhip; it was natural for people who poffeffed fuch fentiments as thefe, to become peculiarly interefted in the education of their children,

and they had the satisfaction of be-
holding their three boys early manifest
the most amiable turn of mind;
Frank, the eldest, had lately recovered
from a dangerous fit of illness, and
as it was near the vacation, his
parents kept him at home until
after the expiration of it.

One morning he entered the study
where his father and mother were
sitting, and requested his mamma's
permission to drink tea with Charles
Hammilton; my dear Frank, said
Mrs. Harcourt, you know I always
derive pleasure from promoting your
happiness, and therefore rest assured,
that when I deny your request, I
have

have fubftantial reafons for it ; but
I really do not think Charles Hammilton a boy whofe acquaintance will
ever do you credit. Not credit !
mamma, why Charles's papa is richer
than mine, he has three carriages,
and he has more money than any
boy in the fchool ; yes Frank, I know
it, continued Mrs. Harcourt, and
it is from his *valuing himfelf* upon
his riches, his carriages, and *his father's
exalted fituation,* that makes me think
him an improper companion for you ;
befides, there are many traits in his
character that are very unamiable,
he is as mean as he is proud ; and
depend upon it, my dear boy, his
heart is incapable of friendfhip : and

let

let me intreat you never to form an
intimacy with any being who you
obſerve deficient in natural affection;
recollect for a moment how very
diſreſpectful Charles conducts himſelf to his father and mother, and
how over-bearing to his brothers and
ſiſters; with what inſolence of manner does he addreſs the ſervants;
in ſhort, he is the laſt boy in the
world I ſhould wiſh you to form an
acquaintance with, and though I do
not expect to have the power of
guiding your affections, yet, I flatter
myſelf, I may be able to direct them;
there is Henry Burton, a boy who
poſſeſſes one of the ſweeteſt minds
and moſt generous hearts that ever
inhabited

inhabited a breaſt; with him, my dear fellow, I could wiſh you to form the ſtricteſt intimacy; a friendſhip with ſuch a character as that would not only be a ſource of pleaſure but improvement, for you would be continually witneſſing ſome amiable trait in his natural diſpoſition, and as example is far more powerful than precept, you would imperceptibly copy the virtues you admired; oh mamma, ſaid Frank, Henry and I have long been friends, and I love him very much, and think he is worth fifty Charles Hammilton's; but Charles can be very entertaining, indeed mamma; you cannot think what a good mimic he is, and how

exactly

exactly he can take off his acquaintance; and can you think Frank, replied Mrs. Harcourt, that you are without imperfections? no, certainly mamma; but why do you aſk the queſtion? becauſe, depend upon it, to the firſt perſon he ſaw after you left him, would he *expoſe* thoſe *imperfections*, and all under the hypocritical appearance of being entertaining; and thus, if your character is not injured your weakneſſes would be expoſed; but if he was to correct theſe faults, replied Frank, you would not then object to my being acquainted with him mamma? I am not apt to take prejudices, replied Mrs. Harcourt, but whenever I am *convinced*

a

a *character* is *bad* I am not eafily perfuaded to believe it will *grow better*,
at leaft when the faults proceed from
the *heart*, and as that is my opinion
of Charles Hammilton, I beg that
all intercourfe between you may
drop ; well, mamma, faid Frank, you
know beft, and fo I will think no
more about this faid birth-day ; but
he is to have a very large party, and
they intend to have a great deal of
fun.

I cannot promife you a great
deal of *fun*, but I think I can offer you
fome amufement, if you will go with
me this afternoon and fee Mr. Par-
kinfon's mufeum ; oh mamma, that is
quite

quite the thing, but do tell me what we are to fee there ? a great deal to delight an admirer of nature, but as I have never been there, I cannot give you an exact defcription ; there are animals, vegetables, and minerals, in high perfection. I dare fay we fhall fee an Elephant, mamma ; and I wonder whether he has got the bird with the flaming wings that papa fo often faw in the Mediterranean ; you know, replied Mrs. Harcourt, that they had only that very flaming appearance when they flew againft the fun. Oh, and thofe little infects which fo frightened the failors, when papa was on the coaft of Malabar ? thofe little infects, if

you

you recollect, your papa told you, were so small that they could not be seen with the naked eye, and that they loft their luminous power when they had been out of the water about half an hour.

A servant now entered and told his master, that Mr. Newman wanted to speak with him ; step down Frank, said Captain Harcourt, and beg Mr. Newman will send word up what his business is, for I am very busy writing letters of consequence ; papa, said Frank, when he returned, they are going to erect a new hospital, and Mr. Newman hopes you will put your name down on this list for there are

are a great many of your friends
whose names are inserted; my compliments to Mr. Newman, replied Captain Harcourt, and I wish his plan
success, but I shall not become a
subscriber; *not* become a subscriber,
papa! why Mr. Newman said he was
sure you would, you were so very
benevolent; I am obliged to Mr.
Newman for his good opinion, continued Captain Harcourt, but as I
have not a very large fortune, I pre-
fer disposing of that part of it which
I allot to benevolent purposes, in
private, rather than in public, chari-
ties; well, but papa, said Frank, this
is only two guineas, come, you had
better give it to him; and with two

guineas

guineas my dear boy; I have been
enabled to impart happine&s to a
whole family who were in hourly expectation of being deprived the comforts of a home by a mercile&s land-
lord, to whom they were indebted
that &um ; &o take the li&t down and
&ay what I de&ired. John again came
up &tairs to inform his ma&ter that
a &ailor of the name of Wilmot
begged to &ee him, I do not recollect
his name, &aid Captain Harcourt, but
let him come up, John.

A young looking man, with a
countenance expre&&ive of the hone&ty
of his heart, now enter the room,
with a &ervant your honour ; mahap
you

you have forgot Joe Wilmot, oh no,
my honeſt friend, replied the Captain, and I recollect that I never had
a better ſeaman ſerve under me, but
where have you been theſe three
years ? pleaſe your honour, ſaid Wilmot, I have been going down in the
world ever ſince I left your honour's
ſhip ; firſt I went to the Weſt-Indies
and there I caught the fever, and had
liked to have tipped the buket, then
coming home, I fell from the top-
maſt and broke my thigh, and when
I was able to go on ſhore and had
got my wages, then a jackanip's of
a fellow, who called himſelf a ſailor
(though pleaſe your honour I do
not believe it) told me a ſad ſtory
with

with fuch a fmooth tongue, that my heart ached for him, fo I offered him half my birth; but the firft night the dog came, he ftole my bag that I kept my money in, and I have never been able to hear of him fince; but the worft is, I now owe my land-lady five and twenty fhillings, and this is worfe than all the reft, for pleafe your honour, I never was in debt in my life before, and this woman's rating at me all day long, with a voice louder than a boatfwain's whiftle; but the long and the fhort of my coming here is, that I hear your honour's got a fhip, and I fhould be glad to ferve you. Why, my brave fellow, you have been

E   going

going *down* in the *world*, indeed; however, we muft contrive to fet you aloft again: and firft of all there is fomething to ftill the clamour of your landlady's tongue, faid Captain Harcourt, laying two guineas upon the table; and as to my fhip, you may enter on board her as foon as you pleafe. God for ever blefs your honour, and all that belongs to you, faid the poor fellow, with an expreffion of gratitude in the tone of his voice more forcible than language; and as to you, madam, faid he, turning to Mrs. Harcourt, I fhall never forget your kindnefs to my poor dear mother, poor foul, fhe ufed to fay you did her more good than

all

all the doctors stuff, and I would work by night and by day to serve you. Thank you kindly, Wilmot, for your good intention towards me, said Mrs. Harcourt, with a smile of ineffable sweetness; and suppose you go down into the kitchen and see some of your old friends, and tell them I desire they will make you welcome.

That man's conduct to his poor mother, my dear Frank, said Mrs. Harcourt, as he left the room, was a pattern to those in much more exalted situations; when she was ill he took a lodging for her close to the place where his ship was situated,

E 2 and

and every moment that he could be
abfent from his duty on board, he
fpent by the fide of her bed; he
never drank his allowance of liquor,
but let it remain until there became
a gallon due to him, which he then
fold, and carried the produce to her,
and his wages he difpofed of in the
fame manner; and when fhe died
his unfeigned grief was really diftref-
fing; and yet much as I fhould have
wifhed to ferve this poor fellow, faid
Captain Harcourt, had I fubfcribed
this morning to the hofpital, I fhould
not have thought it right to have
done it; and why not, papa, replied
Frank, becaufe, continued his father,
if my benevolence is not reftrained
within

within the bounds of prudence, I should reduce myself to a level with thofe I wifh to relieve; well, papa, but you could have taken him on board your fhip; yes, my dear boy, I could have certainly have done him that act of kindnefs, but he would ftill have felt oppreffed with this debt to his landlady; but I would have you remember, that acts of kindnefs are continually coming within the ability of every man, though real benefits we but seldom have the power of beftowing.

Pray mamma, faid Frank, what time fhall we go to Mr. Parkin-fon's?

fon's ? we will dine early and go immediately afterwards. One of our boys, continued Frank, told me there were feveral of the things in the mufeum that Captain Cook brought from Otaheita with him : perhaps, mamma, the elephant came from thence ; no, replied Mrs. Harcourt, the only animals they have are hogs and dogs ; they muft foon be tired of pork, then, faid Frank ; oh, but they have poultry, fifh, and wild foul ; potatoes, yams, fruit, and vegatables, cocoa nuts, and the bread tree, in great perfection, fo you find they are not very badly off. I wonder, mamma, faid Frank, why Omiah could not be happy in this country ?

country? for a reafon my dear boy, that did honour to his affectionate feelings; he had left behind him a father, brothers, wives, and children, and all the gratifications we could offer him were infipid when he reflected upon the delight he had enjoyed with thefe tender connexions! wives, mamma! why had he more than one? yes, fuch is the cuftom of that country, and Omiah, though a very young man, had feveral; well, returned Frank, when I marry, one will fatisfy me, but I intend to love her with all my heart; love her Frank, faid Captain Harcourt, as well as I do mine, and fhe will not have reafon to complain

E 4   of

of your want of affection; yes, papa, said Frank, I think you fet me a very good example; but I wifh dinner was .ready, for I am very impatient to be gone, mamma. At this moment the fervant announced it to be on the table; as foon as it was over, the coach was ordered, and they drove to the mufeum, Frank was fo delighted with all that he faw that he intreated his mamma to promife that he fhould devote a whole day to the infpection of it; and then he is to give me a defcription of all the curious things it contains; which I intend to impart to you for the amufement of fome future evening.

STORY IV.

MR. ADAMS was a gentleman of very large property, which he derived from an extensive share in one of the tin mines in Cornwall; his family consisted of two daughters and a son; the harmony and affection that subsisted between these children was delightful to behold; George, the eldest, was about thirteen, and had been placed at a public school about two years; but Selina and Harriet were educated at home; when

the

the Chriſtmas vacation approached,
Mr. Adams, as uſual, went to fetch
his ſon, and his little girls felt the
livelieſt ſenſation of delight at the
thoughts of embracing their beloved
brother; well, George, ſaid Mr. Adams
to his ſon, as ſoon as the chariot
drove from the ſchool door, and how
much money do you bring away with
you this vacation? not much papa,
replied George ; I doubt you are a
bankrupt, ſaid his father, and at the
ſame time putting his hand into
George's pocket produced ſix ſhillings;
why, I proteſt, here is a perfect fortune!
ſaid Mr. Adams, but how is it that
you, who have hitherto always returned from ſchool ſo poor, ſhould

now

now be fo very rich ? are you going
to turn banker, George ?

I recollect when I was at fchool
there was a boy who ufed to fave his
allowance until it amounted to four
or five fhillings, and then lent it to
thofe who were moneylefs, upon,
condition of their paying him double
after the holidays; the fame boy ufed
to come to fchool loaded like a
pedlar, with tops, bats, balls, whips,
&c. and thefe things, when the boys
returned to fchool with full pockets,
he fold for double their value ; now,
I really have no fear that you fhould
adopt this method, but I confefs
I fhould like to know for what purpofe

pofe you can have faved fix fhillings out of your weekly allowance? well then papa, I muft tell you, that poor Thomas, a very good-natured fervant, who once lived with our mafter, has been very ill; fo ill as not to be able to eat any thing but oyfters, and the boys who all loved him, one, or other, of them, fent him a few every day, but I thought when the holidays came, the poor fellow would mifs his oyfters, fo I determined to fave up my money, and when I got home fend him a barrel; my dear fellow, faid' Mr. Adams, I am delighted with the plan you had formed to gratify poor Thomas's appetite, and you fhall fend

fend him a barrel every Saturday until you return to fchool ; and as I find you intend to make fo good a ufe of your money, there is half a guinea for you to difpofe of as you think proper.

I think, faid Mr. Adams, looking out of the chariot window, it is very fortunate that I came for you to-day, for, from the appearance of the atmofphere, we are going to have a deep fnow; do you know, George, that at Bergemoletto, a fmall village in the vicinity of the Alps, three people were buried under the fnow thirty-feven days, and then dug out alive ; dear papa, faid George, how could that

be

be poſſible ? Why, continued Mr.
Adams, when this amazing maſs of
ſnow, which was driven from the
Alps, overwhelmed the village, theſe
poor creatures were fortunately in a
ſtable ; one part of which being ſup-
ported by a very thick piece of timber, did not give way ; there happened fortunately to be likewiſe in
the ſtable two goats that gave milk,
and though theſe poor ſouls had
hardly room to turn themſelves,
yet it providentially happened that
this ſpot was cloſe to ſome hay, and
therefore, by that means, they had
an opportunity of prolonging the
goats exiſtence, and procuring a degree of ſuſtenance to themſelves juſt
enough

enough to support nature; but when they were difcovered, they were in fo emaciated a ftate that an other day muft have terminated their exiftence.; there were at the fame time thirty houfes overwhelm-ed, and three and twenty inhabitants loft their lives; how very lucky it was, faid George, that the goats were in the ftable; lucky, my dear George, faid Mr. Adams, is not a proper term, it was *providential,* and was ftrongly marking of the protecting hand of a Superior Being. Well, papa, faid George, I am fure there is fomething very lucky, for I can fee my mamma and fifters coming to meet us, and inftantly calling to the
coachman

coachman to ftop, he jumped out of
the carriage and was in Mrs.
Adams's arms in a moment; alter-
nately he embraced Selina and Harriet, and a happier group was never
beheld.

As foon as they got home, they
all went into the play-room, when
George drew himfelf a chair, and
taking each of his fifters on his
knee; now, faid he, tell me all that
has happened fihce I left you; it
feems fuch an age, replied Selina,
that I hardly know where to begin ;
why, you muft begin at the firft
day, replied George : what did you
do after I left you ? what we always

do

do, said Harriet, cried until we gave ourselves the head-ache; the poor dear heads, said George, kissing the forehead of each. Well, the next day? Oh, the next day, continued Selina, that was a luckless one, for I lost the little pocket-book you gave me for a keep-sake; I was quite miserable, for fear you should think I did not value it: but that I am sure I did, though how it went I never could find out. How could you be such a goose to vex yourself about such a trifle, said George, but go on; yes, replied Selina, and how kind do you think dear Harriet behaved about the pocket-book? as soon as she found that all our

F   search

fearch after it was vain, fhe fent Betty out with a new guinea grand-mamma had fent her for netting a purfe, and bought me one exactly like it, and when I awoke in the morning it lay on the table with a little note within fide it, faying, that fhe hoped it would make me fome amends for the lofs of the one you had given me ! fhe is a nice girl, faid George, and always delighted in good natured actions ; yes, replied Harriet, but if you call *that* a good-natured action, what will you fay to poor Selina, walking two miles in the rain to buy me a dove, when one of mine died ! but why did Selina go in the rain, continued George,

George, could she not have waited until it was fine? oh, said Harriet, it did not rain when she set out, but it began soon after, and Betty wanted her to return, but she said she could not bear to see me so uncomfortable; and she did not mind a wet jacket, though she suffered enough for her kindness, for she caught a dreadful cold, and every time she coughed, it went to my heart, for I thought I was the occasion of it; well, said George, and have you been any where, my dear Selina? yes, replied Selina, we have been into Cornwall, and there we saw the poor minors at work, and a shocking employment it is, the poor men all look

so

so dirty and so pale; ah, but, said
George, that is nothing to the mines
of gold and silver and quick-
silver, there indeed you would be
shocked for the poor creatures, are
never suffered to come out; never
suffered to come out, replied Selina,
oh! how dreadful! but why not?
because, continued George, they are
poor wretches who are sent there
as a punishment for some crime, and
they have cruel task masters set
over them, who make them work
without intermission; how do you
know, said Harriet; papa told me
so one day when he had been read-
ing and explaining to me a very
elegant poem written by Mr. Sar-
gent,

gent, called the Mine; well, said Selina, I fhould never have thought of writing a poem upon fuch a difmal fubject; oh, replied George, it is a very pretty ftory that it was founded upon; and if I can I will tell you fomething about it.

At Venice there lived a very amiable nobleman, whofe name was Alberti, he poffeffed fuch a fweetnefs of difpofition, that every one loved the Count Alberti; and the Countefs was very young, very beautiful, and very good; all the foreigners who went to Venice were delighted with this family: well, this unfortunate Count had fome words with a

general

general in the emperor of Germany's
fervice, and they fought, the
general was left for dead, the
Count attempted to efcape, but was
taken and condemned to work in
the quickfilver mines at Idria, to which
.miferable place the poor dear Countefs followed him, think Selina
how fhe muft have loved him; for
though you thought the mines in
.Cornwall gloomy, what would you
have thought of this into which you
are let down in a kind of bucket
more than one hundred fathom, and
the noxious power of the mineral
foon deprives them of the ability to
labour, for they loofe the ufe of
their limbs; well, faid Selina, I am

glad

glad however that the poor Count and Countefs were not doomed to live *long* in fo *wretched* a *ftate*; oh, continued George, I have not finifhed my ftory, there is a great deal of good to come yet; for you muft know the general had only fainted, and when he recovered, application was made to the Emperor to remove the Count and Countefs from their horrid confinement, and they were received with the greateft joy by all their friends and relations; oh, what happinefs, faid both the children: after fuch mifery, it muft be joy indeed, faid George, but I have heard that fome mines are very beautiful mines! beautiful! faid Har-

F 4 riet;

riet, yes continued George, the falt mines of Wielitfka, in Poland, are very fpacious and beautiful, and the reflection of the lamps upon the walls of falt cafts a very brilliant luftre : they have cut feveral fmall chapels out of the falt, and on certain days mafs is performed in them ; but falt mines in general are worth feeing, though the one I have mentioned is by much the largeft and moft profitable.

When you are old enough to go abroad, George, faid Harriet, what wonderful things you will be able to tell us ; yes, my dear Harriet, I fhall have a great deal to entertain you with,

with, but papa tells me, that travel-lers often reprefent things more wonderful than they really are, but I fhall never do *that*, for I fhould be afraid people would never believe me when I related things that were *really true*; befides, when people tell ftories in *little* things, they foon do it in *great* ones; there is a boy at our fchool, who, when he firft came, we liked very much, for he is a generous good- natured fellow, but he is fo dreadful a ftory-teller, that now we have found him out, we none of us can bear to play with him, yet fome of the boys who knew him when he firft went to fchool, told me that then he never ufed to tell ftories only

in

in joke; and who is that, said Mr.
Adams, entering the room, who only
used to tell stories in joke? Charles Turner, papa, replied George, but telling
stories in joke, continued Mr. Adams,
is a very long stride towards the
telling them in earnest; yes, papa,
and that is the case with him, for
he is a sad boy that way, and I was
just telling my sisters so, and besides
he often suffers for faults that he
never commits, for if any mischief
is done and the boy cannot be difcovered he is sure to be blamed for
it, and one day there was some wall
fruit missed and the boys were all
called up; and taxed with having
taken it, however, all denied it, and
the

the blame fell upon poor Charles, and he was ordered to have a fevere flogging, he had received two or three ftrokes, when George Cooper, who had been home for two or three days, came into the fchool, and afking what Turner had done, found he was punifhing for a fault that he had not committed; he called out ftop, and ran to the top of the fchool, and Charles was let down, and George taken up and fuffered the fame difgrace; well, faid Selina, I fhould love that boy, George, though, for his behaviour. Why, my dear girl, faid Mr. Adams, he muft have been a vile fellow to have acted otherwife; there is a great difference

difference between doing our *duty* and the doing an act of *generofity*, if George had been Charles's friend and to fave him from pain, had profeffed himfelf to be the guilty perfon, that would have been an act of generous friendfhip and praifeworthy; but the other was a mere act of juftice ; but, papa, faid Harriet, then Turner would have told a ftory you know ; very true Harriet, replied Mr. Adams, and though I would have a boy of mine a ftrict obferver of truth, yet allowing fuch a motive to have actuated Turner to deviate from it, *that* would induce me to overlook it, for I feel that to ferve my friend, I could fubject myfelf to

any

any inconvenience, and I hope my dear children I shall live to see you all give proof of poffeffing the fame fentiments.

But, I came in, faid Mr. Adams, to propofe a walk to you all, oh, papa, faid the children, we shall like it very much, but where shall we walk too ? why, replied Mr. Adams, your mamma begged me to invite Mrs. Goddard, the Sunday school-miftrefs, and all the little ones, to dinner with us on Chriftmas-day: oh, papa, that is delightful, faid Selina, how happy the little fouls will be ; as they walked along, they faw two or three young lambs, but there

there were not many, as it was rather
too early for them. Papa, said
George, pray does not our sheep
produce more wool than from any
other country ? oh no, replied Mr.
Adams, Spain is the part of the world
where wool is in the greatest abun-
dance ; in short, their sheep walks
are a treasure in themselves. It is
from Spain that we have the finest
oranges, is it not, papa, said Harriet ;
Spain is a very rich country, said
Mr. Adams, it produces in many
places spontaneously the rich fruits
of France and Italy ; but the Spa-
niards are an indolent set of people,
and are very sparing of tillage, or it
would be a very fine corn country ;
they

they have oranges, lemons, almonds, prunes, citrons, figs and raisins, and their wine is excellent, particularly sack and sherry; formerly they had gold and silver mines, but whether they are exhausted, or whether they are too idle to work them, is not known with any degree of certainty; their iron is of a very superior quality, and has always been thought particularly famous for gun barrels. Pray, papa, said George, have they many wild beasts in Spain? no, replied his father, wolves are the only beasts of pray they are infested with. I thought I had heard, papa, said Selina, that silk worms flourished very much in Spain; so they do, continued

tinued Mr. Adams, and their mulberry trees look very pretty loaded
with their produce; I have even
heard that the one article of filk,
amounts to two hundred thoufand
pounds per annum; but it is, you
know, the moft mountainous country
in the world; the Pynenees which
divide France from Spain, are two
hundred miles in length.

The party by this time arrived at
the houfe of Mrs. Goddard, who
received the invitation with delight
and gratitude, and faid fhe was fure
all the little folks would fcarcely be
able to fleep for thinking of the pleafure; a fervant followed Mr. Adams,

to

to fay a gentleman wanted to fpeak with him; well, faid Mr. Adams, if you like to ftay and talk a little with Mrs. Goddard, as you have not feen her for fo long a time, George, you are very welcome, and Thomas may ftay and walk home with you; this propofal was very pleafing to the young folks, and Mr. Adams returned home with all poffible expedition; and now my dear good young ladies and gentleman, faid Mrs. Goddard, cannot you eat a little piece of pie after your walk; for a neighbour of mine, not thinking the 'fquire would be fo kind to me, has juft fent me a large nice minced pie againft to-morrow; oh, no, faid

G.   Selina,

Selina, we would not rob you of it for the world; oh, do not talk of robbing, Mifs, faid the poor woman, for I am fure it will do me more good to fee you eat it, than to eat it myfelf; and according fhe fpread a nice white looking napkin on the table, and produced the pie, which George protefted fhould not be cut, unlefs Mrs. Goddard would divide it in four, and fit down and eat with them, which fhe reluctantly confented to; and pray, Mrs. Goddard, faid George, how many fcholars have you? thirty, Sir, faid fhe, and though I fay it, thirty as good children, and who know their duty as well as any within thirty parifhes of us; and fo

they

they may well, replied George, for I will be bound to fay, you take pains to teach it them; thank you mafter for your good opinion, and I believe the 'fquire and madam too are pretty well fatisfied with them; however, Sir, you will fee them to-morrow, and I hope you will not think I have faid too much in their praife; I quite long for to-mor-row's coming, I affure you, faid all of them, but pray come early; which Mrs. Goddard promifed, and the children took their leave.

As foon as they got out of the houfe, George took each of his fifters by the hand, and faid, I want to afk

your

your advice ; you muſt know, that papa has given me half a guinea, and I have been thinking I ſhould like to ſpend part of it upon theſe children; I ſhould like to call at the bakers and order thirty two-penny plum buns, and when they go away to-morrow evening give one to each ; oh, what a happy thought, they both exclamed, how it will delight them : accordingly they called at the bakers and beſpoke the buns, and then returned home.

Well, papa, ſaid George, as he entered the ſtudy, where is the gentleman who wanted you ? the gentleman, replied Mr. Adams, is in

the

the kitchen, it was your mamma's brother's old fervant, Edward, but what do you think he came for, George? I cannot tell indeed, papa, perhaps to fay my uncle would come and fpend the Chriftmas with us; no, not exactly fo, but to beg that we would fpend it with him; and to intreat that I will fet off to-morrow morning, as he has an old college companion of mine, who muft leave him in a day or two, but who is very de-firous of feeing me. And will you go, papa, faid all the children eager-ly; why, your mamma wifhes it, fo I believe I fhall, replied Mr. Adams; they all expreffed their delight at this in-

tended

tended expedition: oh, but the poor Sunday fchool children, faid George, what will they do? the houfe-keeper, replied Mr. Adams, will attend to them the fame, as if we were at home; that will fettle the affair comfortably, faid George, and away he flew to Mrs. Harrifon to tell her of his plan with the buns, and giving her five fhillings, begged fhe would pay for them.

The next morning the coach was at the door by eight o'clock, when Mr. Mrs. Adams and the children fet out for Moreton Abbey, the feat of Mrs. Adams's brother,

STORY V.

AT a small village in one of the most romantic spots in Cumberland, lived a Mr. Berry, the worthy rector of the parish in which he resided; he was a man that possessed every qualification that could call forth the love and respect of his parishoners, and he was perfectly venerated by them; in Mrs. Berry shone all the milder virtues that could adorn a feminine character; though their fortune was small, yet,

by

by ſtrict œconomy, they were enabled
to do a thouſand benevolent actions,
and the poor never applied for relief
in vain.

Mr. Berry had two ſons, the eldeſt
a boy about fourteen, poſſeſſed a
ſweetneſs of diſpoſition that was
captivating, and to this was united,
a moſt unbounded deſire for the at-
tainment of knowledge; from a child,
he habituated himſelf to reflect upon
every circumſtance that ſtruck him
as wonderful, and this habit had the
happieſt effect in forming his judg-
ment; George, the youngeſt, with a
natural good heart, occaſioned his
parents many hours of anxiety, for
he

he was fo dreadfully indolent, that neither punifhment, or perfuafion, could make him apply, yet his affec- tions were warm, and his heart ten- der; and he always felt a degree of remorfe, when he witneffed the un- eafinefs he occafioned his father; though he had not refolution to cor- rect thofe faults, he lamented poffef- ing; Edward was delighted to im- part to his brother that knowledge he had obtained by application; but if any circumftance was not quite clear to George's comprehenfion, he always doubted the fact; and if the relation ftruck him as at all marvel- lous, he either flatly contradicted the poffibility of it, or walked away hum-

ming

ming a tune, as much as to fay, make me believe it if you can; in fhort, he carried this incredulity of difpofition to the moſt provoking degree, and a temper lefs gentle than Edward's would have been conſtantly teazed by it; but with the moſt philofophic calmnefs, he ufed to try to convince him he was wrong. It was the cuſtom of the brothers to rife early and walk before breakfaſt, and one lovely morning, on the firſt of April, they chanced to ramble to a fpot where two wood-men were engaged in felling a large elm tree, they ſtopped to view the body feparated from the roots that fupported it, and Edward was aſtoniſhed at obferving

obferving a large toad crawl from a
fmall cavity in the folid part of the
tree, and the wood-cutters expreffed
as much furprife, but George perfectly laughed at what he termed
his brother's folly, in believing it
poffible that any creature could have
exifted without the aid of external
air ; why, you goofe, faid he to Ned,
do not you know that it is the firft of
April, and thofe fellows I dare fay
have often heard that you amufe
yourfelf with finding out the virtues
of an old dry ftick, or the qualities of
a flint ftone; and fo they had a mind
to make a fool of you by contriving
to pop the toad in a hole of the tree
that you might puzzle your brain for
a week

a week in conjecturing how it came
there; Ned fmiled at this idea of
his brother's, but as he walked along,
his mind was intent upon tracing
the poffibility of the reptile by any
means having made a paffage to fuch
a fituation; but thought that impoffible, as the tree was perfectly folid;
he determined to apply to his father for
information on that point; and therefore made the beft of his way home
for that purpofe, but George amufed
himfelf with fauntering along, and
throwing ftones into the lake on the
banks of which he was walking;
Mr. Berry met his fons at the end of
the garden, and Ned informed him
of the aftonifhment the fight of a

toad

toad in such a situation had excited;
the circumstance, my dear boy, said
Mr. Berry, is not common, and I
never witnessed it, but I can explain
its cause, for the egg must have fallen
through some of the pores of the tree,
and the creature have been hatched
in that habitation: but when I was in
the harbour of Toulon, I saw a circumstance of a similar nature, which
was no other than small fish of an
exquisite flavour taken out of a solid
mass of stone, and the spawn must
have been laid in the earth, or mud,
of which afterwards the stone was
formed; well, said Mr. Berry, George
do you believe the truth of these circumstances? I hardly know, papa,
replied

replied George, whether I do or not, though if you really *saw* the *fish taken out* of the *stone*, I muft believe it ; perhaps, continued Mr. Berry, as you doubt the poffibility of a toad receiving nourifhment from the fap of a tree, and fifh from ftones, you may not credit a matter of fact which has been well authenticated, and this is no other than that many of our fellow creatures have abfolutley owed their exiftence to a bread made from earth ; for you muft know, that in the German wars, the foldiers were fo dreadfully diftreffed for pro- vifions, that from a hill in Lufatia they formed the earth into bread, for they had obferved, that when the

fun

fun had heated it, it cracked and
fmall white globules of a kind of
meal proceeded from them, and of
thefe they made their bread; and I
have alfo heard that at Catalonia in
Spain, the fame kind of earth is
found; but my dear George, if you
have a grain of affection for me, let
me intreat you to fubdue the natural
incredulity of difpofition, and never
doubt the poffibility of a thing becaufe
you have not capacity to comprehend
it: but fet about improving your
mind, and then circumftances that
now appear wonderful will no longer
be fo, for then you will be able to
trace their courfe; yes, papa, faid
George, but would it not be very
foolifh

foolish to believe every marvellous tale that one heard merely because it was out of the common way; certainly, replied Mr. Berry, but I do not advise that to get out of one extreme, you should run into another: a very credulous character is generally a very weak one; and a very incredulous disposition, is generally united to obstinacy and self conceit; but there is a happy medium between the two, George, which I think with a little pains you might attain; but, I am forgetting that your mother is waiting breakfast for us all this time, and so let us make the best of our way home.

The

! The next morning the boys again left their beds at an early hour, to enjoy their accuftomed ramble, and as they walked on the fide of a hedge they perceived a viper extended in the fhade it afforded, Ned had a thick fhort ftick in his hand, and aiming a blow at it, inftantly laid it lifelefs at his feet; I thought Ned, faid George, you made a point never to take away the life of any creature; neither would I for the world, replied Ned, hurt any thing that was harmlefs, but look at this little bag under its tongue; it contains a poifonous liquor, my dear fellow, that would foon do your bufinefs; for if you had but a flight wound and was to

H   rub

rub the part with it, its effect would
in all probability be the death of you ;
come, Mr. Philofopher, faid George,
do not hum-bug me, that won't do,
for I have heard people eat vipers,
and I would eat that for fix-pence ;
and fo you might very fafely, faid
Ned, if you did not touch the head
part ; and a boy at our fchool told
me, that when his mamma was
thought to be in a confumption, the
phyficians ordered her broth made of
them ; I fhould like however, faid
George, to try whether what you tell
me about the poifon is true, and I
have a great mind to rub a little of
it on my thumb which I cut yefterday ; forheaven's fake, faid Ned, give
me

me the viper, and do not terrify me with the idea of your being fo foolifh. At this moment Mrs. Berry called Edward, and he flew to obey the fummons; no fooner was Ned out of fight than George determined making the experiment, and accordingly rubbed his thumb with the contents of the bag; Mrs. Berry had called Edward to walk with her, to fee a fervant who had formerly lived with them, but who was very ill; George joined the party, but had not walked a great way before he began to feel his thumb very painful; I am fure, my dear George, faid Edward, looking at him, you are not well; do but obferve mamma, he looks as pale as

H 2 death,

death, pale indeed, faid Mrs. Berry, quite alarmed, what is the matter my beloved boy? oh, do not frighten yourfelf mamma, faid George, I am only a little fick, and it will prefently go off. We will return however, faid Mrs. Berry, my love, and do lean upon my arm; let me run on to the apothecary's mamma, faid Ned, for I am fure he is very ill; it was with difficulty poor George could get home, the pain of his thumb was fo intenfe; Ned had found Mr. Freeman at home, and he arrived at Mr. Berry's juft before Mrs. Berry and George; no fooner had he feen his patient than he looked quite alarmed at the appearance of

him,

him, but the moment George con-
feſſed his folly, he deſired Mrs. Betry
not to diſtreſs herſelf, for that there
would be nothing to apprehend if
her ſon conſented immediately to
have the thumb amputated; George
declared he would ſubmit to any
thing without complaining, but that
he ſhould never forgive himſelf for
having been the occaſion of ſuch
terror to his mamma and brother. He
never ſo much as ſaid oh! when the
operation was performed, and whenever George uſed to expreſs his fears
that his hand was in pain, my dear
Ned, he would ſay, do not pity me,
I deſerve ten times more than what
I endure ; but it ſhall be a leſſon

through

through the whole of my life, and fo it proved : for from this period, he fet about conquering the little infirmity of his difpofition and became a very amiable young man.

STORY VI.

AS Mrs. Manfel was one evening pointing out to her children the beauty of the fetting fun, their attention was called from admiring that luminary, by the tears of a child who was bewailing the lofs of a jug, which from, an unlucky accident, fhe had broken; my poor child, faid Fanny Manfel, do not diftrefs yourfelf fo much about the lofs of your jug, I will give you fix-pence to buy another; thank you

H 4   kindly

kindly Mifs, replied the little girl, but I am grieved about the milk, for I do not know where to buy any, and mammy wants it for the poor baby whofe mother is dying at our houfe. Mrs. Manfel, whofe heart was ever open to the emotion of compaffion, inftantly enquired the hiftory of the poor woman; I do not know any thing about her, faid the child, only that fhe is very bad, very poor, and very friendlefs, and it is very fhocking to fee her; oh mamma, faid the children, do let us fend her fome money by this little girl; had we not better go and fee her my dears? faid Mrs. Manfel; no, mamma, replied Fanny, do not let us fee her,

her, for it will shock us so very much;
my dear Fanny, returned Mrs. Mansel, I hope and believe that you
have a feeling heart, but to a
person who did not know you as well
as I do, you would appear to have a
very selfish one, for to avoid the pain
the sight of distress would occasion
you, you are charitable but by halves;
besides, you heard the poor creature
was friendless; and a few words of
symphathy, to such a sufferer, may
be more soothing to her mind, than
all the comforts your purse might
be able to procure her body; indeed,
mamma, said Fanny, I never thought
of that, but I will run directly and try
to comfort her; we will all go, continued

tinued Mrs. Manfel, and this little
girl fhall conduct us to her cottage,
and then fhe fhall buy her jug;
when they arrived at Mrs. Crofts,
I hear, faid Mrs. Manfel, you have an
unfortunate ftranger at your house,
who is very ill, and I am come to
know if I can render her any fervice;
blefs you madam for your kind intention, faid the woman, but the
poor foul, whoever fhe was, wants no
more kindnefs from any of us: but
what is to become of the poor babe
fhe has left behind God knows!
if I could afford it, I would never
part from it; do, faid Mrs. Manfel, tell me who this unfortunate woman was? why, madam,

returned

returned Mrs. Crofts, I will tell you all I know about her : laſt night as I was getting my huſband's ſupper after he came tired from work, I heard a lump againſt our door, what is that John, ſaid I ? ſome unlucky boy or other, ſaid he I ſuppoſe, but never mind him, the next moment we heard a groan, and running to the door, we ſaw a poor young creature lay with a child faſtened round her waiſt, about a month old; at firſt we thought her dead, but I warmed ſome vinegar and held under her noſe, and my huſband he kept rubbing her hands and feet till at laſt ſhe opened her eyes, and ſo then I heated a drop of

elder

elder wine that madam at the par-
fonage house had given me, and put
a little to her mouth, but the poor
foul could not fwallow it : fhe made
a fign for me to put the child on
the bed by her, and fhe preffed it to
her bofom and fighed as if her heart
would brake ; it would have melted a
heart of ftone to have feen her, and
I cried over her like a child. Though
fhe could not fpeak, fhe was very
fenfible ; and when fhe faw how
mortally I was grieved, fhe took my
hand and kiffed it, and then pointed
up to heaven as much as to fay, God
would make me amends for my goodnefs ; but it muft have been a fad
hard heart that would not have

been

been kind to such a young helpless creature; soon after she fell a sleep, and so madam she lay until about half an hour ago, when, she went off like a lamb. I wish I could find out who she was, or were she came from, but she had nothing about her that could inform me, though I am sure she has seen better days; and as to the child, it is the sweetest babe that ever was set eyes on. My good worthy woman, said Mrs. Manfel, though my heart is pained by the sufferings of the poor unknown, it is delighted to find such sentiments of true benevolence in so humble a situation; as for the hapless stranger, I will take care she shall be laid decently in the grave;

grave. And I will endeavour to
supply the place of a mother to
the poor little orphan, for Providence has bleſſed me with an
ample fortune, and I feel a delightful
ſatisfaction when I can relieve the
diſtreſſes of my fellow creatures, and
as you have acted ſo humane a part
by the mother, I am ſure I can
depend upon your acting a tender
one by the child, therefore ſhe ſhall
remain at nurſe until ſhe is old
enough to be received into my
family; when that is the caſe, I am
ſure my children will be happy to
ſhew her kindneſs and affection; oh,
that we ſhall, mamma, they both
replied, and we ſhall never play
with

with our dolls then ; you muft not only play with her, faid Mrs. Manfel, but inftruct her ; indeed, I mean to put her intirely under your care, and you muft work for her alfo; we will work all day long mamma, faid Louifa, to make her comfortable, poor little helplefs thing ; indeed, faid Mrs. Manfel, you muft begin the moment you go home, for fhe muft want clothing, but pray Mrs. Crofts let us fee our little ward, the infant was immediately brought, and while they careffed the unfortunate innocent, they could not help fhedding a tear to the memory of its haplefs mother ; the children told their mamma they had each five

.fhillings

shillings in their purses, which they
requested she would permit them to
spend at the linen-drapers for the
child; this was immediately complied
with, and they returned home with
their bargains, eager to begin upon
their new employment.

When they entered the house,
the footman informed his mistress
that a gentleman of the name of
Selby was in the drawing room—is
it possible !—exclaimed Mrs. Mansel; oh, my uncle—my dear uncle,
said the children, running before
their mamma and embracing him ;
when Mrs. Mansel's joy was a little
abated at the unexpected arrival of

her

her brother; my dear George, said
she, I never suffer my own happiness
to break in upon that of others, and
therefore I know you will excuse me
for half an hour, when I tell you
that I am quite the village doctress,
and that one of my poor patients
has sent to beg to see me; my
dear Charlotte, said Mr. Selby,
pray do not treat me as a stranger,
but follow the dictates of your
own benevolent heart, without having any idea of ceremony; and
Fanny and Louisa must tell me all
they have done and seen in my ab-
sence; I do not think, uncle, said the
children, we shall be able to entertain you much, for we have not

I   seen

feen a great deal, though we are juft now come out of Derbyfhire, as my mamma has been to Buxton for the ufe of the waters; I fuppofe you know, Sir, that the fprings are warm at that place? I never was there, faid Mr. Selby, and beg you will tell me what occafions the warmth; mamma informed me, it was from the waters meeting in their fubterraneous paffage with beds either of coal, fulphur, iron, or amber, all of which are of an inflamatic nature; and fhe faid, that when fhe was at Brofeley in Shropfhire, fhe faw a tea kettle boiled in ten minutes over what they termed a burning well; well, faid Mr. Selby, and what is there remarkable

markable befides thefe warm fprings?
oh, we went to the Peak, and had a
fine view from its top, and we went
to Elden-hole, and there Louifa was
fuch a goofe, fhe was afraid even
to look down it: and we could
not perfuade her to venture into
Pool's-hole; but mamma and I did,
and you cannot think, uncle, how
beautiful the petrified water looked,
as it hung from the fides of the
cavern, when the light from the
guide's candles fhone upon them;
but, I tell you what we have feen,
uncle, which I liked much better
than any thing in Derbyfhire, faid
Louifa, and that was, the King's
Proceffion to St. Pauls; oh, it was

a very

a very fine fight, and every body was
fo happy to fee him well again: for
you know, uncle, every body loves the
King; but I thought it very odd of
mamma; for, when his coach paffed, I
faw the tears fall from her eyes, and
when I afked what occafioned it, fhe
faid *pleafure*; but, for my part, I
always laugh when I am pleafed.

If you like a proceffion, Louifa,
faid Mr. Selby, you fhould have
been with me at Palermo, for you
muft know that the Sicelians have
an annual gala in honour of their
favourite Saint; and on this day fhe
is drawn in the greateft pomp through
the principal ftreets of Palermo in
a triumphal

a triumphal car, feventy feet long
and eighty high; the front is an
oval form, with feats like a play-
houfe, which are filled by a numerous band of muficians; over this
orcheftre is a high dome raifed upon
pillars, on which is placed a large
filver ftatue of the figure of St. Rofolia, the whole is adorned with a
number of Saints and Angels, and
decorated with orange trees, flower,
pots, &c. it is drawn by fifty-fix mules
richly caprifoned, and driven by
twenty-eight poftilions, drefled in
gold and filver ftuffs, with large
plumes of oftrich feathers in their
hats; oh, my dear uncle, faid Louifa,
that I was but St. Rofolia, to ride in

such

such a fine car; well, but this is not all, replied Mr. Selby, for this wonderful procession is succeeded by, the most beautiful illumination you ever beheld, and fire works more splendid than you can imagine, in short, for four days, there is a continuation, and a variety of the most showy amusements; well uncle, continued Louisa, if you love us, and ever go to Palermo again, only ask mamma to let us go with you, for I would give my ears for a sight of that dear Saint who makes so many people happy; I wished for you, I assure you, replied Mr. Selby, and so I did when I walked in the orange groves at Malta, for the fruit is finer than

any

any I ever tafted; I wifh you had brought fome with you then, uncle, faid Fanny; I would have done it with pleafure, my dear girl, returned Mr. Selby, but they are fo lufcious a fruit, and the rind is fo much thinner than the Spanifh oranges that they would have been fpoiled in the journey; however, I brought you fomething from Malta; though, perhaps, not a very elegant prefent for a young lady, but I wifhed to compare them with the Englifh manufacture, for you are to know that the people of Malta pride themfelves upon having brought their cotton ftockings to much greater perfection than any other country; and this

I 4   may

may be accounted for by the different
growth of the plant; plant, uncle!
—why I thought it was a tree—
the cotton that comes from the Eaft-
Indies, continued Mr. Selby, is from
a tree; but at Malta, it is a plant,
about a foot and half high, covered
with pods full of cotton and capable
of being worked into the fineft tex-
ture. I fhould like to go to Malta
very well, faid Louifa, but not half
fo well as Palermo; for my part,
replied Mr. Selby, the impreffion I
felt when I entered the canal of Malta,
will never be effaced from my remembrance; it was one of thofe nights,
Fanny, that I dare fay you have often
heard your mamma admire, the moon
fhone

shone with unusual brightness; and
the lustre of its beams played upon
the smooth surface of the water; the
firmament was bespangled with in-
numerable stars, and the surrounding
coast was wonderfully picturesque,
the sailors were singing the mid-
night hymn to the Virgin, and keep-
ing time with their oars. Well,
Louisa, said Fanny, would not you
rather have been on the canal at
Malta, than seeing the procession of
St. Rosolia? no, to be sure I would
not, replied Louisa, and for one ride
in St. Rosolia's car, I would not mind.
if I never saw moon, stars, or water,
through my whole life.

Mrs.

Mrs. Manfel now returned, well, faid fhe, how much work has been done? are the things almoft finifhed? no, mamma, replied Fanny, we have been attending to our uncle, who has been giving us fome very pleafing information, but now, if you approve it, we will go and work up ftairs, and then we fhall not have any thing to take off our attention ; by all means, faid Mrs Manfel, and pray remember that the poor helplefs babe cannot enjoy the comfort of frefh clothing until your work is complete ; when they got into their apartment, they found Mrs. Manfel's woman and the houfe-keeper very bufy in cutting out complete fets of baby-linen,

they

they therefore requefted their affift-
ance in contriving the things they
had bought, to the beft advantage;
and they all fat down to try who
could evince the greateft kindnefs
to the child, by working the hardeft;
before bed-time, there was a frock,
fhirt, cap and night-gown, quite
complete, and Mrs. Hardy, the houfe-
keeper, fet off with them to Mrs.
Crofts; and the next morning, Mrs.
Manfel promifed they fhould go and
fee the little girl dreffed in them;
the children arofe by fix o'clock, and
when their mamma came down to
breakfaft, fhe was aftonifhed to find
fo many articles complete, in fo fhort
a fpace of time; I hope, faid fhe, my

dear

dear girls, it is not merely from its being a new employment, that you take so much delight in it, but that you will ever feel the same degree of pleafure, whenever you can have the power of fhewing kindnefs to the little orphan; yes, mamma, replied Louifa, that I am fure we fhall; but do pray order in your chocolate, for I am quite impatient to fee it; but you muft endeavour to fubdue this natural impatience of difpofition, Louifa, continued Mrs. Manfel, and by way of giving you an opportunity of doing it, I muft tell you, that the chocolate is not boiled enough, and therefore you cannot go to breakfaft this half hour; I wifh, faid Louifa, they made

chocolate

chocolate as they do tea, but pray, mamma, is there a chocolate tree? chocolate, replied Mrs. Manfel, is a paſte made from the cocoa-nut, which is a tree that flouriſhes in many parts, but I believe it attains the greateſt degree of perfection in the Weſt-Indies; and pray, mamma, is not coffee a ſhrub? coffee is made from the berries of a tree, the chief of it is imported from Moco, a port town in Aſia, or from Grand Cairo in Egypt, and is in itſelf an amazing branch of commerce.—I know mamma, ſaid Louiſa, that ſugar comes out of canes; but I want to know how they manage it? you muſt know then, that the plant riſes about nine

or ten feet high and it is jointed; they
therefore cut the cane from these
joints (and there is very soon a suc-
cession of new shoots from them) and
when they have stripped the reed
from their leaves, they are tied up
in bundles and sent to a sugar mill,
and by the weight of a great roller,
broken in pieces, the juce runs into
pans which are set ready to receive
it, and after a procefs of boiling, it
is put into casks and exported, but
it is refined and made into loaves
after it arrives in England.

. The fervant now brought in breakfaft, and with it a little jar of new
honey, which he faid, Mrs. Crofts
                                        had

had fent, with her duty to the young
ladies; I think, faid Mrs. Manfel, there
feems to be as many amiable points
in that poor woman's character as I
ever met with; that fhe is induftrious,
we may judge from the appearance
of every thing around her; that
fhe has humanity and tendernefs, we
have witneffed, and her little prefent
to you, convinces me fhe is grateful;
but, mamma, faid Fanny, fhould not
we offer to pay her for the honey?
by no means, returned her mamma,
you would fenfibly pain her by fuch
an act, for, depend upon it, fhe is
really gratified by the idea of proving
that fhe is grateful, and fhe means it
as an act of kindnefs to you; you fhall
                                    make

make her amends by giving her something in return, but not for the world
would I have you offer to pay for it;
did I never tell you, continued Mrs.
Manfel, that the bees in Africa, form
their habitation in the hollow of trees,
and that there are people who get
their livelihood by collecting the
honey; in this employment, they are
affisted by a little bird, called the
honey hunter, this little creature,
when it difcovers a ftore-houfe, fits
upon the branch of the tree, and
continues a fhrill note of cher, cher,
until the people arrive, who are in
purfuit of it; they then fly away
to another tree, and adopt the fame
plan; and this is an inftinctive
method,

method, to preferve its own exiftence, for a little honey is always
laid on the branches, by way of
rewarding its diligence; but why,
mamma, faid Fanny, could not the
little honey-hunter fly into the hole
and help itfelf? for the very fame
reafon, my dear, that you could not
put your hand into a bee-hive; when
I think what induftrious, as well as
ufeful, little creatures, bees are, I
cannot help being fhocked when I
hear of children who deftroy them
through mere wantonnefs or cruelty!
but there is no harm in killing wafps?
mamma, faid Louifa; there is
harm in every act my love, faid Mrs.
Manfel, that tends to leffen the feel-

K   ings

ings of compaſſion; and if we can habituate ourſelves to the killing waſps without *reflecting*, that we are *inflicting* an *agonizing pang*, I fear we ſhall have taken one ſtep in the path of inhumanity, yet it often becomes neceſſary to kill them, or their number would hazard our own eaſe.

But now, if you pleaſe, we will viſit our little charge; when they arrived at Mrs. Crofts, they heard the child was quite well, but a-ſleep; they drew back the curtain of the cradle to contemplate the innocence and beauty of its countenance; oh, that it was but big enough, mamma, to live with us, ſaid Louiſa; but what

.is

is its name Mrs. Crofts? that, I do not know Miſs, replied the woman, but I ſuppoſe madam will have it chriſtened; oh, mamma, ſaid the child, do let it be called after me; no, Louiſa, ſaid Fanny, I think it ought to be named Charlotte; oh yes, ſo it ſhall, replied Louiſa; will you, mamma, have it named after you; it ſhall be any name you like, my dear children, for, as I intend you ſhall have a great deal to do with its education, I ſhall let you fix thoſe little points yourſelves. Well, then Charlotte ſhall be its name, Mrs. Crofts, ſaid both the children at once; but, mamma, we muſt make it ſome-thing ſmarter to be chriſtened in, and as it is not awake, do let us go home and begin.

Accordingly, the whole day was devoted to preparations for the chriſtening, and when that was over there was always ſome new employment found neceſſary for little Charlotte, they viſited her every morning, and time increaſed their affection and tendernefs for the little orphan.

STORY VII.

MR. and Mrs. Pennington refided upon a family eftate near Exeter, and devoted their time to the education of their children : Emily, their eldeft, was in her fourteenth year ; and Charlotte was one year younger, and poffeffing one of the moft amiable difpofitions that a child could be bleffed with. Unhappily, Emily, was of a very contrary nature ; fhe was proud to a degree of infufferance, and was fo felfifh,

K 3   that

that all her ideas feemed to center in her own gratification ; in fhort, her heart feemed incapable of a tender or affectionate impreffion. Mr. Pennington had a fifter, married to a gentleman of immenfe fortune, who refided during the winter months in London. This lady, whofe name, was Newton, wrote to Mrs. Pennington, requefting her eldeft niece might pafs part of the winter with her; and that when Emily's vifit terminated, fhe hoped Charlotte might then be permitted to fupply her place. Mrs. Pennington was averfe to this vifit, from the idea, that the magnificence Emily would witnefs at her aunt's might *increafe*

that

that pride she was so anxious to *subdue*; but Mrs. Newton was so urgent in the request, that a refusal was impossible.

When the morning arrived for Emily's departure, Charlotte joined her sister with eyes absolutely swollen with weeping; which Emily observing, said, so, Miss Charlotte, you have been crying, I suppose, because you are not going to see my my aunt, though you know that as I am the eldest I have a *right* to go *first*. No indeed, my dear Emily, your going *first* was quite out of thoughts; but this is, you know, the first time we were ever separated,

and

and I cannot help being pained by it ; but as to going to London, I have no wish, for I am so happy in my dear mamma's company, that I am sure I can never feel so much so in any other persons. What, said Emily, have you been telling mamma this fine canting tale, to make her believe, that your affection is superior to mine? it is very hard, Emily, replied Charlotte, that you will always put such unkind conftructions upon my actions; and juft at the moment we are going to part, it is really cruel!

Mrs. Pennington now entered the apartment, to tell Emily that the chariot

chariot was at the door, and her papa ready to attend her. Charlotte ran up to her fifter, and embracing her with the utmoft tendernefs, faid, fometimes think of me, Emily, and write to me, I intreat you, my dear girl; oh, I fhall make no promife, faid Emily, with the moft mortifying indifference, and giving her a cold falute, ran down ftairs; fhe took leave of her mother with as little degree of tendernefs, and jumped into the carriage with as much joy, as if fhe had not left a fingle dear connection behind.

Mrs. Pennington's heart was exquifitely pained by this proof of indifference,

difference, and the whole day, neither herself or Charlotte could rally, their spirits; the next morning when they were at breakfast, Mrs. Pennington observed Charlotte look very absent, what are you thinking upon, my beloved girl, said Mrs. Pennington? I was thinking mamma, replied Charlotte, how much the poor negro's endure to supply us with this article, (at the same time taking up a lump of sugar) and I have a great mind to leave off drinking it; the little portion of sugar that you drink, Charlotte, can never add to the sufferings of those unhappy people; and besides, they are employed in a variety of occupations, besides cultivating

the

the fugar cane. I wonder mamma, continued Charlotte, how long it is ago, fince flavery was firft allowed? that is a queftion, replied Mrs. Pennington, I cannot refolve, but the period is very far back, for the ftory of Jofeph, in the facred writings, is a proof of it ; but it is a moft difgraceful traffic, and fhocking to human nature ! pray, mamma, faid Charlotte, how are the blacks made flaves of? why, my dear, by a variety of methods, the children of flaves are *fo* by *birth*; for being born in bondage they inftantly become the property of their parents mafter ; and in Africa, the internal ftates make war upon one another, and of

courfe

courfe, the weak become flaves to the ftrong, and thofe poor creatures are then fold to European fhips, that trade to thofe parts. When thefe fhips arrive at the ftated place, they very often fend boats up the rivers Gambia and Senegal, and under the mafk of friendfhip, invite the poor unfufpecting Africans on board, when, inftead of being treated with the hofpitality they expect, they inftantly find themfelves fecured and placed in the moft confined fituation you can imagine. Humanity fhudders at a conduct fo treacherous, and difgraceful ! And think, what muft be the feelings of the haplefs captive, torn from every endearing con-nection—

nection—separated from his country—and condemned to inceffant
labour! but, my dear Charlotte, it is
a subject that pains me even to talk
of, and as it is an evil out of our
power to remedy, we can only lament the neceffity of it ; and therefore, we will turn our reflection to a
more pleafing fubject, and think of
the bleffings that Providence has
benevolently beftowed upon us, and
receive them with grateful hearts.
Yes, mamma, faid Charlotte, it is a
fhocking thing not to be *grateful*;
but pray, fpeaking of gratitude,
what have you ever done to oblige
Mr. Howard the curate fo very much,
for he always feems to think you have
been

been fo uncommonly kind? your father had once the power of proving his friendfhip for Mr. Howard, and he always remembers it, but acts of kindnefs, my dear Charlotte, fhould never be talked of; however, as you mention that worthy man, if you have any inclination for a walk, we will call upon him this morning; oh, I fhall like it of all things, mamma, only I muft juft run up ftairs and fetch down my little magnet, for Charles Howard was fo pleafed at feeing it take up the fteel hat pins, that I am determined to give it him; indeed, I think myfelf, it is very amufing : the magnet, continued Mrs. Pennington, was a moft

fortunate

fortunate difcovery, though I believe I explained to you the utility
it is of to mariners.   Yes, mamma,
I remember all about the compafs,
but I wonder how the power of the
loadftone was firft found out.—I have
heard, replied Mrs. Pennington, that
it was difcovered by a fhepherd ac-
cidentally paffing over fome of the
ore, and having nails in his fhoes,
they were attracted by it, which fo
terrified the poor fellow that he left
them on the hill, running home,
and reprefenting to all the neighbours the moft tremendous account
of what had befallen him ; the circumftance reached the ears of fome
enquiring mind, and by degrees the
whole

whole properties of the loadftone were difcovered.

As they were walking, I think, faid Mrs. Pennington, this is the firft time I have heard the cuckoo, and its note feems the forerunner of the feafon I fo much enjoy. If I was King of England, faid Charlotte, I would have every cuckoo deftroyed, they are fuch vile birds. I fuppofe, faid her mamma, Charlotte, you are provoked at their idlenefs, and exafperated at what you think their cruelty, at leaft I indulged thefe fenfations until I was told by a naturalift, that the cuckoo is fo formed that it would be impoffible

poffible for it to hatch its own young. How is that, mamma? Why, my dear, the ftomach of birds are foft, for the purpofe of fitting upon the eggs; but the breaft-bone of the cuckoo is formed fo different, that it is impoffible for her to fit upon hers; therefore, you know, by a wonderful inftinctive faculty, fhe always watches until fome other bird has formed its habitation, and if fhe finds eggs already in it, fhe throws them out, and depofits her own. Well, mamma, faid Charlotte, is not that wonderful! It is, my dear, replied Mrs. Pennington; but you will find a thoufand things in nature, that, if they call forth

L   your

your aftonifhment, at the fame time mark the directing hand of an all-wife Providence.

Much fooner than Mrs. Pennington expected, fhe received a letter from Mrs. Newton, faying, that as fome friends of hers were going to Exeter, fhe thought it would be a convenient conveyance for Emily, and therefore Mrs. Pennington might expect her the Monday following. She was convinced, from Mrs. Newton never mentioning her behaviour, that fhe had conducted herfelf unpleafingly, and particularly as the vifit was fo much fhortened. As fhe left her friends

without

without regret, fo fhe met them without pleafure ; and fhe had fcarcely been an hour at home before it was vifible her *pride* had been augmented by the fplendour fhe had lately enjoyed. The houfe was paltry, the attendants vulgar, and to be obliged to *walk* into the village would be mifery. At night, when fhe went to bed, fhe was anxious to unpack her box, to fhew Charlotte a pair of pearl ear-rings her aunt had given. When Charlotte had admired them, Betty, who was in the room, faid, will you give me leave to look at them, Mifs Pennington ? You, look at them ! faid fhe, why, you ignorant creature,

you

you don't know a pearl from a
pumpkin. Not quite so ignorant
as that, Miss, said Betty; but as I
really do not know what pearls are,
I shall be glad if you will tell me.
They are, said Emily, in the most
insulting tone of voice, ornaments
proper to be worn by people in my
situation; but I shall not give myself the trouble to explain them any
further to a creature so much be-
neath me. At this moment Mrs.
Pennington entered the room, having, from an adjoining one, overheard the preceding conversation;
she instantly demanded the ear-
rings, and turning to Betty, said,
these baubles shall never more be

the

the occasion of your being treated
with a degree of impertinence, I am
shocked at having heard ; and then,
addressing herself to Emily, said, I
expect you first to ask Betty par-
don, and then explain where pearls
come from. She did the first in an
ungracious manner, but when she
was again desired to give Betty the
information she wished for, she be-
gant hesitating, pearls—pearls—oh,
I had forgot—pearls are dug out of
the earth. Mrs. Pennington shook
her head, saying, I am shocked at
your pride, and hurt by your ignorance. But do you, my dear Charlotte explain it. Pearls, said Charlotte, looking at Betty with a con-

descend-

descending sweetness of countenance,
are taken out of oysters; there are two
seasons in the year, in which the pearl
fishery is practised, the one in March
and April, and the other in August
and September. The divers go out
in little barks before sun-rise, and
when they arrive at the rocks, they
tie a flat stone round their waist, and
another to their foot, which occasion them soon to sink; they fasten
a large net round their necks by a
long cord, which is fastened to the
bark; this cord is to pull up the
diver when his net is full, or he
wants air; the best divers will keep
under water half an hour, and the
rest a quarter; when they return,
they

they lay the oyfters into a number of little pits, four or five feet fquare, and cover them over with fand; in this ftate they continue until they open and the oyfter decays; the rub-bifh is then cleared out, and the fand carefully fifted to feparate it from the pearls. Betty thanked Charlotte for the hiftory; and Mrs. Pennington, taking the ear-rings with her wifhed them good night.

The next morning ordering the chariot, fhe drove to a jeweller's at Exeter, and difpofing of the ear-rings (which were made of fmall pearls, and of courfe not very va-luable), with the money fhe bought

L 4 a coarfe

a coarfe ftraw hat, black fhoes, and coloured gown, for Emily, and the remainder of the fum fhe laid out in books. Upon her return, fhe found the children dreffing for dinner, and ordering Betty to bring up the feat of the chariot, fhe faid, it contains, Emily, cloathing for you. Emily was eager to fee it opened, but when the contents were expofed, her countenance was expreffive of anger and difappointment. Surely, mamma, faid fhe, you can never mean a daughter of your's to wear cloathing only fit for a cottager! Indeed but I do, replied Mrs. Pennington; for as your pride was increafed by ornaments, I hope the

plainnefs

plainnefs of your apparel will teach
you humility; and if this leffon has
not the defired effect, depend upon
it, Emily, that the happinefs of our
family fhall not be deftroyed by
daily witneffing your unamiable conduct; for my determination is fixed,
and I am refolved to fend you to
School far diftant from us, where,
poffibly, when you find yourfelf deprived of thofe tender indulgencies
you have always met with at home,
you may learn to prize thofe bleffings
you hitherto have fet no value upon

STORY VIII.

AS Mr. Lumley and his fon Herbert were feated under the
branches of an extending oak, to
fcreen themfelves from the fcorching
rays of a noontide fun, they overheard
two boys, on the other fide the hedge,
converfing very warmly upon a point
they differed about—I tell you what,
Jack, faid one to the other, if you
do not take my advice, and carry the
purfe to the crier, that we may find
out who it belongs to, though you
and

and I have been friends thefe four years, I will never have any thing to fay to you again; for you might as well *fteal* a purfe, as keep one without enquiring who has loft it. Why, replied Jack, I never heard of fuch a fcrupulous fellow; is not what I find my own? and I am fure my father is poor enough; and thefe three guineas would go a good way towards buying him another cow, to make amends for ours that died the other day; however, you have preached fo much about its being a fin and a fhame, Bob, that I will even go with you to the criers, and let the money be hanged; for I would not do a BAD *action* any more than you, though I

did

did feel tempted to keep it ; that is
right my honeft lad, faid Bob, giving
him at the fame time a hearty clap
upon the fhoulder, and away they
both ran. .

What a leffon, my dear Herbert,
faid Mr. Lumley to his foh, might
the converfation we have juft overheard teach you; yes, papa, faid Herbert, Bob is a very good boy, indeed,
but Jack, you heard was inclined to
keep the purfe ; true, replied Mr.
Lumley, and what a comfort it is
for him, that he has chofen for his
friend, a boy older than himfelf, who
is able to advife him; and, at the
fame time, poffeffing fentiments that
                                    might

might do honour to the moft exalted
ftation ; and, I think, this a good opportunity to inforce the neceffity
there is for your being very particu-
lar, as to the character of the boy
with whom you enter into habits of
intimacy.

I am not apprehenfive, my dear
fellow, that your own heart, if you
followed its dictates, would lead you
into error; but with fo eafy, and at
the fame time, fo attached a difpofition, as yours, if you were unfortu-
nately to form a connection with a boy
of an unamiable turn of mind, I
fhould tremble for the confequences,
as I fear he might lead you into the
road

road of vice, before you were aware that you were verging to its path.

This converſation was interrupted by the arrival of Mrs. Lumley, and her daughter Charlotte ; oh ! Herbert, ſaid Charlotte, we have got a holy-day to-day, for my governeſs has juſt heard that her ſiſter is married and the young ladies are going to have a very nice entertainment, but I preferred coming home; for though I love them very much, I love you my dear brother a great deal better ; and beſides, I wanted to tell you ſomething.

You

You muſt know, that poor Joe Turner, our gardener, is lately dead with the ſmall-pox, and has left a wife and five ſmall children; the poor creature is in the greateſt diſtreſs imaginable, for they have for a long time been very unfortunate; their children have all been ſickly, and Suſan herſelf ſprained her wriſt ſo bad, that ſhe was unable to work; ſo my governeſs has ſet a ſubſcription on foot in the ſchool, and we have got five and thirty ſhillings for her; and upon my ſaying, I thought my mamma would add ſomething to it, my governeſs gave me the money, and deſired, that if my mamma was ſo kind as to contri-

bute

bute, that I would call and give it the poor creature, as fhe has never had the fmall-pox, and does not like to go to the houfe. Well, faid Herbert, taking out his purfe, let me fee how much I can give the poor foul; oh, I can very well fpare two fhillings, continued he; but let us go to mamma, and tell her all about it. Mrs. Lumley applauded the benevolence of her children, and adding five fhillings to the fum, gave them leave to carry it to Sufan; they inftantly flew acrofs the church-yard to the cottage; they found the poor creature in a very reduced fituation, extreme poverty was depicted in the appearance of

herfelf

herfelf, and children, and her countenance was the index of a wounded
heart ! She was chopping onions, by
way of thickening water gruel for
the childrens dinner, when they
entered ; Sufan, faid Charlotte, how
do you find yourfelf ? we are come
to bring you a little comfort, oh,
Mifs, replied the unhappy woman,
I doubt not, comfort and I have
long been ftrangers, and I fear we
fhall never be friends again; do not
think fo, faid Herbert ; though we
have all our troubles in this world;
papa often tells me; but you know,
Sufan, they will all end by and by;
yes, replied Charlotte, we fhall all
be happy, you know, Sufan, when we

M   go

go to heaven; but there is something to make you comfortable before hand, faid fhe, laying down the
two guineas upon the table; my
governefs raifed it by fubfcription,
and my mamma added five fhillings
to it, and bid me tell you to come to
dinner every Sunday.   Heaven blefs
you! my dear young lady, faid the
poor woman, and reward you for
your goodnefs, to an unfortunate
widow, whofe prayers will ever attend
you! the children left the cottage,
with the moft delightful fenfations of
fatisfaction, from having been inftrumental to the happinefs of a
fellow creature, and ran eagerly
home to impart the account of the
fituation

fituation they found the poor woman in.

My dear children, faid Mrs. Lumley, as they entered the room, why have you ran in that violent manner? you look in a perfect fever; indeed Charlotte, faid Mr. Lumley, you muft not pay your uncle a vifit in India, if a day like this put you into fo great a heat. Papa, faid Herbert, we will fit down comfortably and cool ourfelves, if you will have the goodnefs to tell us fomething about Bengal; but pray, papa, firft inform me why it is called India? from the river Indus, replied Mr. Lumley. And as to Bengal,

it

it is fo very abundant, that it is ftiled the ftore-houfe of the Eaft-Indies ; the produce of the foil confifts of rice, fugar-cane, corn, fefamum, fmall mulberry, and other trees, and its muflins, callicos, filks, falt-petre, wax, and civit, are exported to every part of the world: provifions of all forts are in vaft plenty, and very cheap ; the principal Englifh factory is at Calcutta, and is called Fort William ; a moft melancholy cataftrophe happened there in the year 1756, when one hundred and forty-five Britifh fubjects were forced into a confined prifon, called the Black Hole of Calcutta, about eighteen feet fquare,

and

and out of that number, only twenty-
three came out alive, the reft endured
the moft agonizing death from fuffo-
cation.

About four miles from Bombay
(which is an Englifh fettlement) is
a very curious ifland, called the ifland
of Elephanta, which derives its
name from the figure of an Elephant,
hewn out of a maffy ftone, and fo
exact a reprefentation of that animal
is it that you would take it for a
living one ; as you afcend a hill, you
arrive at the portal of a cavarn formed
out of a folid rock, the entrance of
which ftrikes you with the appearance of a magnificent temple, about

M 3   ninty

ninty feet long by forty broad ; at the end of this temple, are three gigantic figures, . of moſt excellent workmanſhip, though I could not find that they had any relation to any part of hiſtory ; but upon the whole, this place is vaſtly well worth feeing, and the Engliſh often make parties and ſpend the day there.

I ſhould be afraid, papa, ſaid Herbert, ever to go out upon a party of pleaſure, if I lived in the Eaſt-Indies, for fear of the tigers ; for do not you remember Mr. Howard telling us a ſtory of a number of his friends who were dining under a tree, and that a tiger was juſt going to make

a ſpring

a fpring at a lady, who luckly had the prefence of mind to unfurl an umbrella at him, the furprife of which, fo terrified the animal, that he walked away; yes, replied Mr. Lumley, I recollect the ftory, but happily people who refide there, do not fuffer their minds to be continually dreading an evil that may never happen. Well, papa, continued Herbert, but the heat of the climate would be very difagreeable to me; for I love cold weather better than hot, and I would rather live at Kamchatca than Bengal; there is no accounting for tafte, Herbert, faid his father, but I think if you knew what boorifh beings the poor

M 4

in-

inhabitants of that country are, you would not be very fond of affociating with them. Pray, papa, faid Charlotte, where is Kamchatca, for I never recollect hearing any thing about it. It is, replied Mr. Lumley, fituated in the north-eaft extremity of Afia, and is a country but little known ; the natives of it are as wild as the country itfelf ; fome of them have no habitation, but wander about with their herds of rein deer, and form temporary dwellings upon the banks of the rivers, living upon fifh, fea animals, and fuch herbs as grow upon the fhore ; their huts are formed by digging a hole in the earth about

five

five feet deep, the breadth and length proportioned to the number of people who are to inhabit it; in the center is the fire-place, and round the sides are placed benches, on which the family sleep, and the walls are adorned with mats made of grafs; they are dirty in their perfons to a difgufting degree; their clothes are made of the skins of deer, dogs, and several sea and land animals; their dogs differ very little from our common house dog, and in travelling, they generally yoke four to a sledge; but it is very difficult to travel in these sledges, for unless a man keeps the most exact balance he is every moment subject

to

to be overturned, for the roads are very rugged, and the dogs never ftop until they come to fome houfe, or are entangled by fomething on the road. If a ftorm of the driven fnow furprifes them, they are obliged to feek the fhelter of fome wood, or dig a place under the fnow, or hide themfelves in holes of the earth, covering themfelves with fkins.

Before the arrival of the Ruffians in Kamchatca, they ufed ftones and bones inftead of metals; of thefe they made hatchets, fpears, arrows, needles, and lances; in order to kindle a fire they ufe a board of dry wood with a hole in it, and in this they

they turn a ftick fo rapidly, that it takes fire, and for tinder they fubftitute dried grafs. For want of proper timber and plank they fometimes make their boats of the fkins of fea animals, and they conveniently hold two people.

The hiftory of the Kamchatdales was interrupted by the entrance of a fervant, who prefented Mr. Allen's compliments to Mr. Lumley, and fhould be happy if himfelf and family would accompany him that afternoon in a fifhing party. The children intreated their father to accept the invitation, and it was immediately determined that the carriage fhould should be ordered to convey them to the banks of the river. Herbert was eager in collecting the fishing-tackle, and in less than an hour from the time the message arrived they all entered the coach with the highest expectation of enjoying good sport.

STORY IX.

THE next morning, as Mr. Lumley was at breakfaft, a meffage was delivered from Mr. Frampton; requefting half an hour's converfation with him. I will wait upon him immediately, faid Mr. Lumley, and finifhing his cup of tea, inftantly left the room; mamma, faid Herbert, what was the reafon that we could none of us perfuade you to fifh yefterday? becaufe, replied Mrs. Lumley, it is an amufe-

ment

ment I could not receive fatisfaction from, for I can never feparate the idea of the pain, the poor little victim fuffers, from the pleafure I fhould derive from the fport; but then, mamma, why did not you tell Mr. Allen fo, when he preffed you fo earneftly to join in the amufement; why, continued Mrs. Lumley, had I given Mr. Allen my reafons, Herbert, he might either have 'thought that I carried my humanity 'to a degree of affectation, or that, I 'might fuppofe, that by his enjoying 'the amufement fo thorougly, he was 'devoid of that amiable principal, 'and thefe unpleafant ideas were both 'avoided by my filence; then mam-

ma

ma, replied Herbert, you think fifhing a very inhuman employment;
no, my dear boy, *inhuman*, is much
too ftrong a term; but I confefs
that I have fo great an averfion to
the giving pain, that I always fhrink
from the very idea of it, and as there
are fuch a variety of diverfions, that
can never call forth any unpleafant
fenfations, I would wifh you to make
choice of thofe in preferance; for
any amufement that tends to leffen
the feelings of humanity in a young
mind, I difapprove, and the fame
reafon actuates me to hope, that I
fhall never fee you fond of courfing,
for the purfuing a poor little timid
creature, with power fo much fuperior

perior to its own, feems to me, at once barbarous, and cowardly; however, if you have a mind to become a fox-hunter, the fame objection does not exift, for they are voracious animals, and their deftruction is to be wifhed for; I do not think mamma, replied Herbert, I fhall ever become a fox-hunter, for I cannot help feeling in a fright, when I am on horfe-back; that is for want of more practice, continued Mrs. Lumley, joined to your having had a fall; but you muft conquer fuch a ridiculous fear, or you would be laughed at; a cowardly girl, is a filly being, but a *cowardly boy* is *defpicable.* I am *not cowardly,*

mamma

mamma, faid Herbert eagerly, with his face glowing at the idea of being fufpected of fuch a weaknefs; and I only wifh I had an opportunity of *fhewing* you my *courage*. Well, faid Charlotte, who had hitherto fat filent, I know that I am exceffively *terrified* at the fight of a moufe. Terrified at the fight of a moufe! replied her mamma; never, Charlotte, let me again hear you expofe yourfelf by fuch an expreffion; thofe ridiculous alarms are always the effect of folly or affectation, and I hope you will be fuperior to both; I can't tell you how contemptible an idea all thofe little childifh fears will occafion people to form of your

N   under-

underſtanding; beſides, they would become a continual ſource of un-eaſineſs to yourſelf, and of trouble to thoſe about you; but all thoſe whims I ſhould certainly treat as a diſeaſe, and make you drink valerian tea by way of ſtrengthening your nerves. I think, mamma, ſaid Char-lotte, to avoid ſuch a remedy, I ſhould ſoon try to get the better of the diſeaſe; and I aſſure you, the next mouſe I ſee I will try and ſtand ſtill, and look at it, inſtead of run-ning away. Do ſo, replied, Mrs. Lumley, and in time I ſhall expect to ſee you a perfect heroine.

Mr.

Mr. Lumley now rejoined the party, but with a gravity of countenance that evinced he had been receiving some unpleasant information. I am sure, said Mrs. Lumley, addressing him with solicitude, something has happened to give you uneasiness. Yes, replied Mr. Lumley, and I am doubly pained by the idea, as I know it will occasion you much concern; for could you have believed that Herbert was capable of becoming a story-teller, a thief, and a deceiver!—Impossible! exclaimed Mrs. Lumley; my boy's heart is incapable of it! You recollect, continued Mr. Lumley, about a month ago, hearing that

Mr.

Mr. Lawrence's cherry-ground had been robbed, and that as it joined Mr. Frampton's garden, his boys were fufpected ; accordingly they were all taxed with it, and were obliged to give an account how they were employed when it happened ; for Lawrence was in the garden juft before, and juft after, the theft, there-fore they muft have watched him very narrowly, and Herbert affured his mafter, that he was at the time playing cricket, but it is now dif-covered that he was one of the party.

I intreat, however, faid Mrs. Law-rence, that you will allow him to

endeavour

endeavour to vindicate his conduct as far as he is able.

I should rejoice, if I thought he could say any thing to palliate such an offence, replied Mr. Herbert; but as he has once told an untruth he may, perhaps, impose upon us with some forged tale.

I can bear any thing, papa, said Herbert, but your thinking me capable of *deceiving you* and my *mamma*; and though I own I have been blamable, I hope, when I have told you all, you will not think me so very guilty.

N 3

I shall

I shall rejoice to alter my *present* opinion, continued Mr. Lumley, therefore, desire that you will give me this account, but mind that you do not in the slightest degree, deviate from truth.

Herbet suppressed his tears, and proceeded; on the afternoon, papa, that Mr. Lawrence's cherry-tree was robbed, I was playing at cricket, when George Gorden sent a boy to say he wanted me; when I came to him he told me, that there was a very fine cherry-tree loaded with fruit, in Mr. Lawrence's garden; and that by standing on our pales, we might get at least a dozen pounds from it, and

and as he loved me better than any boy in the fchool, I fhould go halves with him, if I would ftand and catch the fruit, as he threw it over the pales; I told him, I would have no hand in it, for that it would be an abfolute theft ; he was then very angry, and vowed he would never be my friend again ; I was grieved at this, and could not help crying (for I love him dearly) but ftill I would not join in the plan ; till George faid, well Herbert, I am refolved upon having the cherries, and as you will not receive them for me, why I muft go and get a bafket, and very likely when I am attending to that, I may not mind where I fet

my

my foot, and so may tumble down and break my limbs, but you will not mind that; for I am sure you no longer *love me*, or you would not refuse so trifling a request as holding a few cherries for me.

I could not bear, papa, to think of his having his limbs broken, or that he should suppose I did not love him; and so I did catch the cherries, but I never eat one, and as soon as he came down I went to cricket again, and so when Mr. Frampton enquired how I had been spending my time, it was no untruth to say, at cricket.

You

You have Herbert, faid Mr. Lumley, taken a perfect load from my mind, by this defcription ; yet I muft highly difapprove your conduct, for the moment George Gorden perfuaded you to act *contrary* to *right*, that moment you ought to have renounced him for your friend. True friendfhip, my dear boy, is a paffion that elevates the mind ; and the boy who poffeffes that noble fenfation, would much fooner commit a fault himfelf, than be inftrumental to his friend's doing it. I little thought yefterday morning, that the converfation we overheard would be fo applicable to my fon; but reflect how much better a poor

cottager

cottager conducted himself than you
have done ; for he told Jack, that
unlefs he immediately endeavoured
to difcover to whom the purfe be-
longed, though he had been his
friend for four years, yet he would
never fpeak to him again. However, as I truft the impreffion of
this leffon will not eafily be effaced
from your mind, I fhall drop the
fubject, only begging, that you will
wait upon Mr. Frampton immediately, and repeat the account I
have juft heard.

No, papa, replied Herbert, I
can't obey you fo far ; I would fub-
mit

mit to the fevereft punifhment rather than do it.

Not go and explain the circumftance to your mafter! faid Mr.
Lumley, in aftonifhment; and what
may be your motive, pray, Sir, for
not doing it?

Becaufe I think, papa, he is quite
angry enough with George already,
and if I was to tell the whole truth,
he would be much more fo; and
though he was very wrong about
the cherries, he is in general a very
good boy; and I am fure you would
defpife me, if, to fave myfelf from
punifh-

punifhment, I could expofe the faults of my friend....

- You are very right, my dear fel-low, faid Mr. Lumley, though the thought did not ftrike me when I propofed your explaining the motive of your conduct to your mafter; but ftill I muft inforce the neceffity there is for your difcontinuing a habit of intimacy with George Gordon, for depend upon it, that boy wants prin-cipal; you may be upon terms of civility with him as a fchool-fellow, but never, my dear boy, confider him as your friend; but we will drop the fubject, and I muft tell you, my dear, faid Mr. Lumley, addreffing

addreffing his lady, that I have juft received a letter from Mr. Herbert, our boy's god-father, intreating us to fpend the remaining part of the fummer at Mucrufs-Houfe. Oh, papa, faid Charlotte, what delight that would be, for I have heard you fay, 'tis a beautiful place; it is certainly, replied her father, one of the fweeteft fpots in nature, and as you have a tafte for drawing, Charlotte, you might there indulge it with advantages that you could receive in no other part of Ireland: you have a moft charming view of the Lake of Killarney, and the Mountain of Mangerton, and the grandeur and magnificence of the

scene,

scene, is more striking than I can describe. In one part, you will see the gay verdure, blended with scarlet fruit, and snowy blossoms, which are the well known properties of the arbutas; and in other places, you would behold the most elegant variety of brown and yellow tints from other kinds of trees and shrubs, and all these are intermixed with rock work; in short, the whole forms a scene to captivate the mind; you would likewise see the iron-works and copper-mines, both of which are at a very small distance from the seat of my friend And will you Papa, said Herbert, accept my godfather's invitation? If your mother

has

has no objection, replied Mr. Lumley, to the propofal, I affure you I
have none, but if we vifit that country, I fhould wifh to fee as large a
part of it as my time will allow;
therefore, we cannot begin our
journey with eagernefs. I have
many things that require my attention at home before I could leave it
for a long period. Well, but furely
papa, you can compleat every thing
in a week, faid Charlotte, for I am
fo delighted at the thoughts of going
that I don't believe I fhall fleep a
wink until the time arrives. At the
expiration of the time Charlotte
named, Mr. Lumley had fettled all
his domeftic concerns, and the family

mily all reached Holyhead, in high health and fpirits, where we fhall leave them to embark for Ireland.

STORY X.

ONE winter's evening, when my four little friends and myfelf had formed a comfortable circle round the fire ; do, faid the children, have the goodnefs to tell us a ftory this evening ; indeed, I replied, I believe you have exhaufted my whole ftock, I pofitively cannot recollect one ; oh, replied the eldeft, you promifed to inform me how you became acquainted with Mrs. Pemberton, who you have fo great

O a regard

a regard for, as you faid it was a fin-
gular circumftance; you are to know
then, I continued, that one fummer
I hired a little cottage in the neigh-
bourhood of Windfor, and one morning as I rambled along the banks of
the Thames, I obferved a lady fitting with two lovely children; there
was a fweetnefs in the tone of her
voice as fhe addreffed them, that
quite captivated me; and I walked
on, wondering who the interefting
group were; and meeting my friend,
Mrs. Onflow, I defcribed them with
the idea that fhe could give me the
information I was anxious to obtain;
it is, fhe replied, Mrs. Pemberton,
for I have juft paffed her; and who

is

is Mrs. Pemberton? I continued, for I am not apt to be caught by outward appearance, but I never felt so strong a desire to form an acquaintance with a stranger; she is, continued Mrs. Onslow, the wife of an officer whose regiment is quartered at Windsor, but I do not think you have much probability of forming an intimacy with her, for she is of a very domestic turn, and devotes the chief of her time to the education of her children; and also seems rather averse to forming new acquaintances, which I lament, for her manners are so very pleasing, that every body wishes to know more of her.

O 2   When

When I got home I was puzzling to think of some scheme to get introduced to this lady, when a melancholy event brought about the wished for circumstance, for my servant entered and told me a most shocking circumstance had happened to a poor woman near us—John Miles, madam, said she, the poor man who lives just by, where 'squire Barnet is building his new house, went about half an hour ago, to the pond, to water one of the 'squire's horses ; when not knowing there was a hole in the middle of it, ventured to the spot, the animal making a false step, threw his rider into the hole; the dreadful shriek, the poor

poor fellow gave, the moment he
saw his danger, reached the ears of
his wife, and flying to the spot, she
juft faw the head of her husband
rifing above the water; poor foul!
fhe fnatched up a long pole, and
running with it into the pond,
threw one end to the fpot where he
was, and kept the other in her hand,
but oh, madam! think what the poor
creature muft have felt, when fhe
faw him juft in the act of grafping
at the pole, fink, and rife no more!
the artlefs manner in which my
fervant told the ftory, and the affect-
ing circumftance inftantly drew forth
tears of compaffion.; but reflecting
a moment, that by haftening to the

ſpot, I might, perhaps, afford ſome relief to the ſufferer; I told Nanny to conduct me inſtantly to the cottage ſhe had deſcribed.

The poor man had been taken out of the water about ten minutes and was apparently lifeleſs; the wife was hanging over the body in ſpeech-leſs agony ! whilſt a lovely little boy, of two years old, was pulling the flap of his father's coat ; and ſaying naughty daddy, not to open his eyes, and look at poor mammy ! this diſtreſſing ſcene, for a ſhort ſpace of time, ſo wholly ingroſſed my at-tention, that I had not obſerved Mrs. Pemberton, who I now ſaw buſily bufily employed in fpreading warm afhes upon a bed in one corner of the room; I inftantly joined in the office, and fending the neighbours who were now flocking into the room, to fetch afhes from their refpective fires, we inftantly undreffed the poor foul, and covering the body with the afhes, and making a free circulation of air, by preventing the people from crowding round the bed, in lefs then a quarter of an hour we had the delightful fatiffaction of perceiving the breaft heave with a fort of convulfive motion; and, before fix o'clock in the evening, the happy wife had the felicity of feeing her hufband reftored to her

affectionate

affectionate arms ; to defcribe the joy and gratitude of this worthy woman would require an abler pen than mine ; it was every thing that can be conceived by hearts, as fenfible of kindnefs as her own, and we left this worthy pair with a fenfation of delight never to be forgotten.

As we were returning home, I could not refift the inclination I felt to improve the opportunity chance had given me of forming a farther acquaintance with Mrs. Pemberton, I therefore told her, that circumftances like thofe we had juft witneffed, brought on an acquaintance between people of a very different nature,

nature, to thofe produced by acci-
dental meetings, in crowded circles ;
and that if fhe would abolifh ceri-
mony, and take her tea with me that
afternoon, it would afford me a
lively fenfation of pleafure, fhe
affured me, that fhe was that moment
going, to make me the fame requeft ;
and that fhe trufted I would comply,
with it, when fhe told me that fome
family occurrences had obliged Mr.
Pemberton to be abfent from his
regiment for fome time, and that
fhe had left her children to the care
of fervants, which was an unufual
thing with her, as they were con-
ftantly either with their father, or
herfelf ; l accordingly agreed to the
                              propofal,

propofal, and from that day entered
into a habit of ftrict intimacy with
Mrs. Pemberton, which, I truft, will
terminate but with my exiftance.

Upon our entering the houfe, the
children flew to embrace their
mother, whilft fhe received and
returned their careffes with the moft
maternal tendernefs. Eliza and
Caroline, eagerly enquired where fhe
had been ? and upon her defcribing
the fcene fhe had witneffed, their
eyes overflowed with fenfibility ;
when taking Eliza by the hand, my
dear girl, faid fhe, I am much pleafed
with this tendernefs of your difpofition, but always let your feelings lead

you

you to endeavour to remove, or lessen, the affliction of your fellow-creatures; for your sympathy, unless guided by that motive, would render you a useless member of that society, you might, by an active degree of benevolence, become an ornament to; for, said she, suppose upon my hearing the accident that had befallen John Miles, I had sat down and wept over the sufferings of his wife; how different would my sensations have been to what they are at this moment; but the instant I was acquainted with the circumstance, I recollected having read an account of ashes having been used with great utility in similar cases; and you

know

know how happily I have fucceeded; and had I not, I fhould have had the fatisfaction of knowing that I had made the attempt, to be ufeful!

But my dear Caroline, faid Mrs. Pemberton, looking at the child, who was putting a fmall box into her pocket, what can you have got there? which, if I may judge by your countenance you did not wifh me to obferve: a little degree of embarraffment was vifible in both the children; come, faid her mother, fhew it me my love, furely you are not going to prove to me Caroline, that you no longer confider me as your friend! and *confidence* is the *foun-*

dation

dation of *friendſhip* !—oh, mamma, ſaid Caroline, I cannot bear that you ſhould talk to me ſo! but ſome how, I do not like to ſhew you this box, becauſe, mamma, though we did not mean to do wrong, ſomething tells me, we have not done right, and I fear alſo, giving you pain. This prelude to the delivering up the box, called forth a thouſand apprehenſions in the breaſt of Mrs. Pemberton, and deſiring Caroline, not to keep her any longer in ſuſpence, the child opened it, and emptying its contents on the table, diſcovered ſeveral ſnails with their heads cut off. Surely, ſaid Mrs. Pemberton, turning from the poor reptiles, ſuch a barbarous em-

ployment

ployment as this, can never have been the amufement of children, whofe hearts I believed fufceptible of every humane impreffion !

Explain to me Eliza, the motive that could actuate fuch an unheard of piece of cruelty? Eliza now approached her mother, and with the utmoft timidity of countenance attempted to take the hand of Mrs. Pemberton, which fhe inftantly withdrew, defiring to be made acquainted with the caufe of the painful fcene fhe had before her.

The children were fo thoroughly diftreffed by the difpleafure vifible

in

in their mother's countenance and manner, that they inftantly fell on their knees before her, and befought her to look at them as fhe ufed to do. We will bear any punifhment, mamma, faid they, you think we deferve, without repining, if you will but let us think we have not loft your affection! Indeed, my dear, dear mamma, faid Caroline, we fhall certainly die if you continue to look at us with fuch averfion.

No, Caroline, faid Mrs. Pemberton, you would not die; but as I believe you are very forry for having difpleafed me, I wifh you immediately to endeavour to exculpate yourfelves

yourfelves as far as you are able; I therefore again desire an explanation.

Why, mamma, the other afternoon, when Mifs Melford was here, we amufed her by repeating fome of the hiftories of living animals, that you have fo often told us; and we informed her, that when our papa was in America, he was purfued by a black fnake, and that after running at leaft two miles he was at laft overtaken by it; that the creature twifted irfelf round his body, but that having one arm at liberty, he had taken a knife out of his pocket and cut off its head, though

not

not until it had given him a fevere
bite, but that it very foon healed
again. Oh ! faid Mifs Melford, cut-
ting off the creatures head, would
do it no injury, another would very
foon grow ; another head grow !
faid I, in aftonifhment ; yes, replied
Mifs Melford, I know it is either
fnakes, or fnails, whofe heads grow
after they are cut off, but now I
think of it, I believe it is the latter;
and I am determined to try the experiment ; it will be a very cruel
one, I replied ; not at all, faid
Mifs Melford, for the head is con-
nected to the body by a membrane
as free from fenfibility as our nails,
and this I was told by a gentleman

P

who

who I can depend upon. Hearing
this mamma, we went into the garden, as foon as you went out this
afternoon, and collected the poor
creatures whofe appearances fhocked
you fo much ; and, though we believed what Mifs Melford told us,
yet we felt a very painful fenfation,
when we feparated the head of the
firft, and put our ear clofe to it, to
hear if it made any noife, or expreffive of pain ; but finding it did not,
we believed we might purfue the employment, and were juft come in,
when you arrived.

I am delighted, my dear children,
faid Mrs. Pemberton, taking a hand
of

of each, to find you have not been fo very blameable as I at firft appre-hended; but reft affured, that the poor fnails have fuffered the fevereft torture, and that the whole of the circumftances are untrue; in the firft inftance, the ftory of the head growing again, is a fabulous idea, as has been proved by the experience of thofe who have repeatedly made the trial, though hundreds of thefe poor reptiles lives have fallen a facri-fice to it. But a gentleman who was determined to difcover whence the idea arofe, obferved, that by cut-ting off the heads of thefe poor crea-tures with a blunt inftrument, which was drawn rather flowly along, the

P 2

fufferer

sufferer had time to contract, or withdraw their heads; so that only the skin with a small part of the head was cut off. However, thus much has been proved, that snails will live a considerable time, after their heads are separated from their bodies.

But, my dear children, I am persuaded that when you have heard this story, you thought the experiment would not meet with my approbation, or you would have acquainted me with it; but, however, we will drop a subject that has occasioned us all so much uneasiness; you, from having suffered my displeasure, pleafure, and me, from thinking that my beloved girls were capable of an act of cruelty. And as you are fond of experiments, I underftand there is a boy at Windfor, at this time, who has the wonderful faculty of dif-covering water under ground; there-fore, to-morrow morning, we will contrive fome excufe to bring him into the garden to fatisfy ourfelves of the truth of the report,

The next morning, Mrs. Pember-ton, defired the gardener to dig a large hole two feet deep, into which he was to put a large earthen pan filled with water, and covered over with another; the grafs was then

laid

laid down again over the part, and the boy, as by chance, was invited to walk in the garden, Mrs. Pemberton, for fome time, led him from the fpot, but returning by another way, paffed over the ground where the water was funk. The boy was walking carelefsly with his hands in his pockets, when coming to the fpot, he ftamped his foot and faid, " Here is water, but it does not run." My aftonifhment was not to be expreffed, which was heightened by obferving, he was in other refpects very illiterate. He was a Portuguefe, and his father poffeffed the fame wonderful faculty.

At

, At this moment a fervant entered with the tea equipage, and a fmall table and tea things upon it, was brought in for the children; Caroline, who was rather inclined to be in a buftle, ran up to it, and in fo doing, overturned the jug of milk. Indeed Caroline, faid Mrs. Pemberton, I believe I muft fend you to Japan, to be taught to make tea gracefully; to Japan, mamma, faid Caroline! Yes, faid Mrs. Pemberton, the children are there taught it as an accomplifhment, in the fame manner as Europeans are dancing, &c. Pray mamma, faid Eliza, does the tea grow on a tree, or a fhrub? and where does it flourifh moft? It is

a fhrub,

a shrub, replied Mrs. Pemberton, which in about seven years, grows to the height of a man, it is then cut down, which occasions an exuberance of fresh leaves and shoots ; it is chiefly cultivated in China and Japan, it delights particularly in vallies, on the declivities of hills, or upon the banks of rivers where it enjoys a southern aspect.   There is great care required in gathering the leaves, which are all pulled one by one, from the stalk ; public buildings are erected for the purpose of drying them, and these buildings contain from ten to twenty small furnaces, about three feet high, each having at the top, a large flat iron pan,

pan, bent up a little on that fide which is over the mouth of the furnace, which prevents the leaves falling off. There is alfo a long low table, covered with mats, on which the leaves are laid, and rolled by workmen, who fit round it. This procefs is repeated two or three times, that the moifture of the leaves may be thoroughly diffipated, and they curl more thoroughly preferved..

Pray mamma, faid Eliza, is Japan near thofe famous cities that were deftroyed by the eruption of Mount Vefuvius? My dear foul, faid Mrs. Pemberton, you make me blufh by expofing your ignorance of Geography:

phy: Japan, is a large empire in the moft eaftern part of Afia, confifting of feveral iflands; the principal of which is Japan, and gives the name to the reft. And Herculaneum and Pompeii are not far diftant from Naples, a kingdom in the fouth of Italy. And what had you told my fifter about Herculaneum? faid Caroline, for I never heard a word of it. That is your own fault, replied Mrs. Pemberton, for you certainly were in the room; but you were fo attentive to the account of the luminous infects made ufe of by the Indians, before the difcovery of candles, that you did not regard what I was faying. I told your fifter, my dear.Caroline,

that

that when I was at Italy, I visited those two wonderful monuments of the destructive power of that liquid fire, called Lava; under the torrent of which was buried these once flourishing cities. The modern discovery, of which, was made by the sinking of a well in the year 1706. I was present at the digging up of several human skeletons that were adorned with gold-rings, ear-rings, and bracelets. The buildings are all in wonderful preservation, and the theatre is in a beautiful stile of architecture.

Near the theatre is a temple, supposed to be dedicated to Hercules, the walls of which are covered with paintings, done in a superior stile of excellence.

excellence. How fortunate it is for us mamma, faid Eliza, that we do not live in a country fubject to fuch dreadful accidents. Yes, my dear girl, replied Mrs. Pemberton, it is fo, for we doubtlefs enjoy more real bleffings and fewer inconveniences in this happy ifland, than in any other part of the globe. At this moment, my fervant arrived, to fay that I was particularly wanted at home, I therefore reluctantly took my leave of this amiable family, but my dear children, as I have informed you how I became acquainted with Mrs. Pemberton, I may poffibly for the amufement of fome future evening, give you a farther account of her children.

F I N I S.

www.ingramcontent.com/pod-product-compliance
Lightning Source LLC
Chambersburg PA
CBHW030114030726
47498CB00007B/2384